A Disturbance in the Dandelions

Tom stood just inside the door, twisting his white panama in his gnarled hands. His rumpled silver hair suggested he'd snatched the hat from his head in a hurry. Felicity stood at his side, a flush of red staining her cheeks.

"I asked him what he wanted," she said, as Meredith paused in front of them. "The silly fool won't say a word."

Meredith could tell something h___ ___hly agitated the elderly gardener. His gaze roamed ___ ___ ___acious, polished floor of the lobby as if seeki___ ___ ___ome troubling question. "Tom, is there ___ ___ ___ell me?"

His gray eyes fo___ ___ ___ide as his mouth trembled. ___ ___ ___ed his bony, sun-scorched ___ ___ ___

"Out wh___ ___ ___g wrong with Miss Duncan?"

Instead of ___ ___sed his hat in both hands and pressed it to ___

"Oh, for heave___ ___e." Felicity stood in front of him and spoke each word as though she were dictating to a dull-witted secretary. "Where . . . is . . . Miss . . . Duncan? What . . . does . . . she . . . want?"

Tom shook his head and his wild gaze sought Meredith's face.

"Show me," Meredith said sharply.

Tom scurried out of the door. Meredith followed his lopsided gait across the lawn.

She saw the crumpled heap of clothes long before she reached the rockery. Fearing the worst, she hurried forward, passing Tom in her haste. Kathleen still wore the dark blue skirt and lace waist she'd worn to supper the evening before.

For a moment Meredith stood transfixed, shock rendering her unable to think or move. Felicity reached her first, uttering an unladylike oath as she took in the scene. . . .

HIGH MARKS
for
MURDER

Rebecca Kent

BERKLEY PRIME CRIME, NEW YORK

THE BERKLEY PUBLISHING GROUP
Published by the Penguin Group
Penguin Group (USA) Inc.
375 Hudson Street, New York, New York 10014, USA
Penguin Group (Canada), 90 Eglinton Avenue East, Suite 700, Toronto, Ontario M4P 2Y3, Canada
(a division of Pearson Penguin Canada Inc.)
Penguin Books Ltd., 80 Strand, London WC2R 0RL, England
Penguin Group Ireland, 25 St. Stephen's Green, Dublin 2, Ireland (a division of Penguin Books Ltd.)
Penguin Group (Australia), 250 Camberwell Road, Camberwell, Victoria 3124, Australia
(a division of Pearson Australia Group Pty. Ltd.)
Penguin Books India Pvt. Ltd., 11 Community Centre, Panchsheel Park, New Delhi—110 017, India
Penguin Group (NZ), 67 Apollo Drive, Rosedale, North Shore 0632, New Zealand
(a division of Pearson New Zealand Ltd.)
Penguin Books (South Africa) (Pty.) Ltd., 24 Sturdee Avenue, Rosebank, Johannesburg 2196,
South Africa

Penguin Books Ltd., Registered Offices: 80 Strand, London WC2R 0RL, England

This is a work of fiction. Names, characters, places, and incidents either are the product of the author's imagination or are used fictitiously, and any resemblance to actual persons, living or dead, business establishments, events, or locales is entirely coincidental. The publisher does not have any control over and does not assume any responsibility for author or third-party websites or their content.

HIGH MARKS FOR MURDER

A Berkley Prime Crime Book / published by arrangement with the author

PRINTING HISTORY
Berkley Prime Crime mass-market edition / June 2008

Copyright © 2008 by Doreen Roberts Hight.
Cover art by one by two.
Cover design by George Long.
Interior text design by Kristin del Rosario.

All rights reserved.
No part of this book may be reproduced, scanned, or distributed in any printed or electronic form without permission. Please do not participate in or encourage piracy of copyrighted materials in violation of the author's rights. Purchase only authorized editions.
For information, address: The Berkley Publishing Group,
a division of Penguin Group (USA) Inc.,
375 Hudson Street, New York, New York 10014.

ISBN: 978-0-425-22204-1

BERKLEY® PRIME CRIME
Berkley Prime Crime Books are published by The Berkley Publishing Group,
a division of Penguin Group (USA) Inc.,
375 Hudson Street, New York, New York 10014.
The name BERKLEY PRIME CRIME and the BERKLEY PRIME CRIME design are trademarks belonging to Penguin Group (USA) Inc.

PRINTED IN THE UNITED STATES OF AMERICA

10 9 8 7 6 5 4 3 2 1

If you purchased this book without a cover, you should be aware that this book is stolen property. It was reported as "unsold and destroyed" to the publisher, and neither the author nor the publisher has received any payment for this "stripped book."

To Bill,
for giving me the gifts of love and laughter.

Acknowledgments

Producing a book is team work, and I'm fortunate enough to work with the best team out there.

My astute editor, Sandy Harding, who so diligently guides my hand when my brain fails to connect with my keyboard, and whose patience, support, and expertise are invaluable to me.

My agent, Paige Wheeler, who never fails to encourage, advise, and make me feel important, even if I'm not.

My lifetime friend Ann Wraight, who provides me with fascinating research and tidbits impossible for me to find on my own. Thank you, Ann.

My fellow author Edie Hanes, who sympathizes when I whine, applauds my achievements, and understands what it is to be a writer.

The incredible art department at Berkley, who always interpret my vague descriptions and produce exactly what I had in mind. Their covers are phenomenal.

My wonderful readers, who enjoy my books and take the time to tell me so. Your notes give me so much pleasure.

My husband, Bill, who is everything I want and need.

I am indeed blessed.

Chapter 1

Under normal circumstances Meredith Llewellyn enjoyed the Sunday services at St, Edmund's. Reverend Geoffrey Wright had a mellow voice, and once in a while his sermons actually made sense.

The hymns were always a pleasure to sing, and after a week of trials and tribulations as headmistress of Bellehaven Finishing School, Meredith relished the peaceful tranquillity of the surroundings. That particular morning, however, she entered the crowded church with an eerie sense of impending doom.

Having rarely paid attention to such pranks of the mind, she made an effort to shake off her disquiet as she took her place between her colleagues. Her resolve faltered when she noticed the empty space in front of her.

Every week, Kathleen Duncan arrived early to claim her seat in the front pew. Meredith couldn't remember a Sunday morning without the familiar sight of frothy peacock feathers waving gently from the wide brim of Kathleen's hat. Since the vicar's wife had already sat down at the organ, it would appear the service was about to begin. Had all been well, Kathleen would most certainly have arrived before now.

Clutching her hymnbook in both her gloved hands, Meredith reassured herself. Kathleen had seemed perfectly well the evening before. She'd joined the rest of the tutors for supper, spouting complaints about a pupil's ineptitude for distinguishing weeds from flowers. Most likely she had slept late and would arrive, breathless and apologetic, in just a few moments.

A loud blast from the organ pipes jolted Meredith out of her musings. The musician's enthusiasm greatly outweighed her talent. In spite of the odd mangled chord, however, the majestic tones echoing in the soaring rafters helped Meredith forget her worries. The sight of brightly hued sunlight pouring through the stained glass windows often served to remind her of the centuries that had passed inside the illustrious walls.

The church must have looked then much as it did today, she thought. As if time had stood still. Yet in the years between, thousands of wedding ceremonies had taken place inside the ancient limestone walls, and indignant babies had wailed at countless christenings.

Now here they were, already five years into the twentieth century. Hard to believe. She still caught herself starting to write eighteen hundred instead of nineteen. Then again, she had trouble accepting the fact that she had passed her thirtieth birthday.

Time was such an intangible thing, swift to pass when looking back, yet sometimes interminable when trapped inside her classroom at Bellehaven.

Aware that her companions had opened their hymn-books, Meredith hastily flipped pages as she rose to her feet. One more glance confirmed that Kathleen still hadn't arrived. Meredith did her best to drown her concerns in the familiar phrases of the hymn. The voice on her left made it difficult.

Although younger than Meredith by five years, many people mistook Felicity Cross for the elder of the two, most likely because she did everything with gusto. She wore her auburn hair scraped back in a bun, and her angular face with its prominent nose could conjure up the fiercest frown imaginable.

She sang and talked louder than anyone else, walked faster than any woman Meredith had ever met, and had a complete disregard for fashion. Since her profession demanded that she set an example for her pupils, these traits were a distinct disadvantage.

She did, however, possess a vast knowledge of literature and could speak three foreign languages fluently—a skill much sought after by the future debutantes. Out of the four instructresses at Bellehaven, Felicity's voice had the most control over the often wayward novices.

Meredith winced as the sour notes chimed in her right ear. On the other hand, Esmeralda Pickard's soft-spoken tones often proved a blessing, since she had no voice for singing.

The youngest of the tutors, Essie had recently turned twenty-one. Her wasp waist and blond curls accentuated her flair for style, and an aristocratic upbringing made her a valuable contributor to the Bellehaven girls' education in the social graces.

The absent Kathleen, who taught home management with a no-nonsense attitude that sometimes made her seem austere, had served at Bellehaven the longest. Since

Meredith's duties also included the instruction of fine arts,
she relied a great deal on Kathleen to help her keep things
running smoothly—a not so simple task when governing
fifty exuberant young women.

Once more she glanced over at the empty pew. Only now
it was no longer empty. White peacock feathers seemed to
float above Kathleen's hat, and the gown she wore had a peculiar sheen to it. Wondering why she hadn't seen her friend
pass by her, Meredith blinked . . . and blinked again. Kathleen had vanished.

A mere trick of the light, Meredith assured herself.
Anxiety over the tutor had caused her to imagine things
that weren't there. Nevertheless, a fluttering of misgiving
troubled her midriff. Afraid that Kathleen might have suffered some kind of illness, she became impatient with the
long sermon that followed.

"Whatever is the matter with you this morning?" Felicity hissed at her later as they filed out of the church into the
blinding sunlight. "It isn't like you to fidget so. Is something troubling you?"

"It's Kathleen." Meredith paused to pay her respects to
the vicar waiting in the porch. "Lovely sermon," she assured him. "Quite inspiring."

He nodded and smiled, though she was quite sure he'd
noticed her lack of attention.

"What about Kathleen?"

Before Meredith could answer her, Felicity's long stride
had taken her to the gate and out of earshot.

A steady stream of young girls poured down the steps,
some sedately mindful of their headmistress as they passed,
while others jostled each other in their eagerness to be out
in the fresh air.

Chattering voices and ringing laughter echoed over the

faded gravestones as the pupils surged through the gate and spilled out into the road.

"Kathleen wasn't in church," Essie said, panting a little as she hurried to keep up with Meredith's quick steps.

"Yes, I noticed that, too." Meredith lifted her skirts to step over a puddle left by a dawn shower. "I find that somewhat disturbing."

"What's disturbing?" Waiting by the gate, Felicity's ferocious frown wrinkled her brow.

"I was just saying that Kathleen wasn't in church." Essie came to a halt by Felicity. "Really, do you have to walk so fast? I'm quite out of breath."

Ignoring her, Felicity scowled at Meredith. "What's the matter with Kathleen?"

"I really don't know" Meredith gave her a worried smile. "It's not like her to miss the Sunday service."

"More than likely overslept." Felicity opened the gate and charged through it, narrowly avoiding a collision with a stout gentleman on the other side. Treated to a sniff of disapproval, she tossed her head and turned her back on him. "Kathleen must have come in very late last night from her walk. I usually hear her pass my door, but I fell asleep before she came to bed."

Felicity's words only deepened Meredith's concern. "I shall look in on her the moment we arrive back at Bellehaven," she said.

"I'm quite sure she'll be up and about by then." Felicity stomped down the road toward the honey-colored roofs of the village.

St. Edmund's had stood sentinel on a hill overlooking the village of Crickling Green for centuries. Nestled in the heart of the English Cotswolds, the churchyard afforded a spectacular view of the village and beyond, where rolling hills thick with sheep overlooked flower-studded grass-lands.

Bellehaven House lay on the other side of the village square. Once the grand home of a nobleman, it had been purchased by an enterprising gentleman and turned into a select finishing school for young ladies.

The staff of Bellehaven were charged with taking raw adolescence and fashioning it into a fabric of maturity, grace, and refinement. At times the challenge could be overwhelming, especially since many of the pupils would rather chain themselves to fences in protest for women's rights than walk across a room with a book on their heads.

While Meredith fully sympathized with the suffragettes and their cause, at times she despaired of some of her students ever becoming ladies. Still, somehow the transformations eventually took place, and she could pride herself on the knowledge that her efforts and those of her colleagues had not been wasted.

With rare exception, every young woman left Bellehaven equipped to face the critical and often vindictive world awaiting her. Though watching the playful sparring of some of the girls occasionally raised doubts.

Half an hour of brisk walking brought Meredith and her fellow tutors to the gates of the school. After making sure all her charges were safely inside the grounds, she followed the women through the gates. By the time Meredith had securely fastened the latches, Felicity had stalked up the curving driveway.

Usually Meredith enjoyed the walk up to the main building. Bellehaven's gray walls glowed in the morning sun, providing a perfect background for the ornamental gardens. Flanked on either side by tall poplars swaying in the breeze, she could listen to the heartfelt song of the thrushes while savoring the fragrance of lilacs and late summer roses.

Today her uneasiness would not allow her to enjoy the heavenly scents. Essie chattered at her side as they approached the thick oak doors at the top of the steps. Meredith paid scant attention.

After returning from church on Sunday mornings, Kathleen would linger in the gardens to instruct Tom Elliot in the placement of her latest bargains from the flower market. Or at the very least chide the gardener for failing to remove the weeds from her beloved flower beds.

Meredith could see no sign of her friend or even the gardener in the main gardens. The reason became apparent when she entered the cool vestibule.

Tom stood just inside the door, twisting his white panama in his gnarled hands. His rumpled silver hair suggested he'd snatched the hat from his head in a hurry. Felicity stood at his side, a flush of red staining her cheeks.

"I asked him what he wanted," she said, as Meredith paused in front of them. "The silly fool won't say a word."

Felicity had no patience for what she perceived as stupidity. Being a little more charitable, Meredith was inclined to make allowances.

True, Tom took longer than some to grasp the gist of a conversation, and his memory often failed him at the most inopportune moments. Nevertheless, he worked hard and possessed an uncanny knowledge of the plant world. In Tom's eyes, all plants were living, breathing creatures to be tended to as one would children.

None of that mattered for the moment, since Meredith could tell something had highly agitated the elderly gardener. His gaze roamed over the spacious, polished floor of the lobby as if seeking the answer to some troubling question.

The feeling of foreboding deepened in Meredith's chest. "Tom, is there something you want to tell me?"

When he didn't answer, she touched his arm. His gray eyes focused on her, growing wide as his mouth trembled with the effort to spill out words. "M-miss Duncan." He waved his bony, sun-scorched arm at the door. "Out there."

"Out where, Tom? Is there something wrong with Miss Duncan?"

Instead of answering, he raised his hat in both hands and pressed it to his mouth.

"Oh, for heaven's sake." Felicity stood in front of him and spoke each word as though she were dictating to a dull-witted secretary. "Where . . . is . . . Miss . . . Duncan? What . . . does . . . she . . . want?"

Tom shook his head and his wild gaze sought Meredith's face.

"Show me," Meredith said sharply.

Tom ducked his head and scurried out of the door.

Meredith started to follow, and Felicity called out after her, "Shall I come?"

"And I?" Essie echoed. She'd been standing in the shadows so quietly Meredith had forgotten she was there. "Come if you like," she called out over her shoulder, then saved her breath to follow Tom's lopsided gait across the lawn.

She saw the crumpled heap of clothes long before she reached the rockery. Fearing the worst, she hurried forward, passing Tom in her haste. Kathleen still wore the dark blue skirt and lace waist she'd worn to supper the evening before. Meredith found that particularly ominous.

For a moment she stood transfixed, shock rendering her unable to think or move. Felicity reached her first, uttering an unladylike oath as she took in the scene.

Seconds later, Essie joined them, and immediately emitted a piercing scream that shocked Meredith into action. With Essie's wailing sobs ringing in her ears, she bent over the still form.

A dark pool of blood stained the rock beneath Kathleen's head. Her eyes were wide open and stared sightlessly at the sky, while her outstretched arms hung limp and lifeless.

Tom stood at a distance, mumbling to himself as Meredith straightened.

"She must have fallen and hit her head," she said, fighting back the resurgence of her breakfast.

Essie's wailing rose in a painful crescendo.

"Is she dead?" Practical as ever, Felicity always came straight to the point.

"I'm afraid so." Meredith suppressed a shudder. "She feels cold and stiff to the touch."

Essie moaned and sank to the ground, causing Tom to stagger backward with a hand over his heart.

Felicity muttered something under her breath and bent down to shake Essie's arm. "Come on, you silly goose. Get up. You're making a fool of yourself in public."

Essie moaned in response.

Somewhat reassured, Meredith turned to Tom, who stood gasping for air like a goldfish deprived of water. "Send one of the stable lads to fetch Dr. Mitchell, if you please, Tom. Then find Reggie. I believe he's in the cellar, attending to a leaking water pipe. Tell him to bring a blanket out here."

Looking relieved to be excused from the scene, Tom loped off.

"It's a bit late for a doctor." Felicity knelt at Essie's side, flapping a hand back and forth in front of her face. "After all, he's not going to bring Kathleen back to life, is he."

Essie moaned and closed her eyes.

"We can't just leave her here." Meredith struggled to clear the cloud of confusion that seemed to fog her brain. "I think the best thing to do is for you both to get back to the school and make certain the girls don't wander out here." She glanced at the building, half expecting to see a crowd of anxious young women charging toward her. "We really don't need a mass panic on our hands."

"I feel sick," Essie announced.

"Up!" Felicity roared, as she leapt to her feet. Reaching down, she grabbed Essie's hand and pulled her upright.

Swaying and pale as death, Essie blinked back tears.

Felicity took a firm grip on her arm. "Are you coming with us?"

Meredith shook her head. "I'll stay until Reggie gets here with the blanket. He can wait with Kathleen until Dr. Mitchell arrives. Then I'll come back and address the school. Would you please ring the bell and take roll call. I want to make sure everyone will be in assembly when I make the announcement."

"Of course." Felicity took the sniffling Essie by the arm. "Will you be all right out here alone?"

Meredith sighed. "As all right as anyone can be."

Felicity spared the inert body a brief glance. "Poor Kathleen. We shall miss her."

"We shall indeed." Unwilling to reveal how shaken she felt, Meredith chose a large rock to perch on. "Arrangements will have to be made, of course, but that will have to wait until later. Right now the important thing is to gather all the girls in assembly."

To her relief, Felicity took the hint and strode off, half dragging Essie with her.

Left alone, Meredith wished she'd brought a shawl out with her. In spite of the sun, the air felt cool and damp. She hoped Dr. Mitchell would arrive soon. Keeping company with a dead body was not a pleasant way to spend the morning.

Out of the corner of her eye she saw a flash of white among the trees. Nervous that one of the pupils might have wondered close enough to see Kathleen's body lying there, Meredith jumped to her feet.

The sunlight filtered through the branches and cast shadows between the thick tree trunks. Again she saw something move—a wisp of white that seemed to float like a puff of smoke. Then it vanished, leaving her with a cold chill that had nothing to do with the moist air.

Chapter 2

Shaken. Meredith seated herself again on the rock. The shock of Kathleen's death had caused her mind to play tricks. She needed a good strong cup of tea. That would settle her nerves. Though coming to terms with the tragedy would require more than hot tea.

Kathleen Duncan had been the first person to welcome Meredith when she'd arrived at Bellehaven. The trauma of losing her husband in the Boer War had caused Meredith to miscarry. Still grieving for both her husband and child, she had sought to alleviate her loneliness by joining the staff of a school.

Bellehaven had been recommended to her by a friend of her late husband's and Meredith had taken some time to consider the idea. The prospect of teaching young women how to conform to the rigid rules of high society disturbed her. She had long been an advocate of the women's movement, even though her husband's military career had prevented her from taking an active part in it.

Nevertheless, the opportunity to introduce to these young women the idea that they had a choice in their future appealed to her. Women were generally schooled in the belief that it was their duty to attend to their home and their husband. Meredith held the opinion that the world would be a far better place if women were allowed to have a hand in running it.

As her colleague, Kathleen had understood the delicate balance it required to obey the dictates of the school board and still maintain her own beliefs.

Just then a shout from across the lawn shattered her thoughts. Reggie Tupper, Bellehaven's youthful maintenance man, headed toward her carrying a bundle under his arm.

He stopped short when he caught sight of Kathleen's body. "Strewth!" He edged closer for a better look. "I thought Tom was daffy when he said to bring you a blanket. Is she a goner, then?"

Meredith flinched. Reggie was not known for his sensitivity. For the most part she could overlook his brashness, but she could not allow him to be disrespectful to her friend in that manner. "I regret to say Miss Duncan has passed on. I would appreciate it if you would cover her with a blanket and please refrain from any more coarse remarks."

Reggie's gaze shifted away from her. "Sorry, Mrs. Llewellyn. Wasn't thinking, was I."

"You certainly were not." Meredith stole a last look at her friend. "Miss Duncan will be sorely missed by us all. She was a fine lady and a dedicated teacher."

"That she was, m'm," Reggie murmured. He shook out the white blanket and covered Kathleen's still body. "That she was, indeed. May she rest in peace."

The threat of tears caused Meredith to blink, and she shook her head. "Thank you, Reggie."

"Entirely my pleasure, m'm."

Rising to her feet, she smoothed the folds of her navy blue skirt. "Dr. Mitchell will be here shortly. I'd appreciate it if you'd stay here until he arrives." She glanced at the mound of blanket. "I really don't want to leave her here alone."

"I understand, m'm. You can depend on me."

Past experience had taught Meredith the opposite, but she refrained from saying so. She was about to leave when Reggie added, "So what do you think happened to her then?"

"Miss Duncan enjoyed walking through the gardens in the late evening. It was her favorite time of the day. She liked to listen to the night chorus of the birds." Meredith let out her breath on a long sigh. "I imagine she tripped over something, and hit her head when she fell."

Reggie glanced around him. "Could have been this branch." He pointed at the ground. "It would have been hard to see in the dusk."

Meredith followed his gaze. "I hadn't noticed that." She looked up at the tree overhead. "It looks like a dead branch. It must have broken off."

Reggie kicked at it with his toe. "Nah, it's been sawed off. Look, the end of it is as clean as a whistle."

"Tom must have sawed it off." She frowned. "I wonder why he left it lying there. He's usually so particular about cleaning up everything."

Reggie didn't answer. He appeared to be studying the branch with an intent expression that unsettled her.

"What is it?" she asked sharply.

"Unless I'm much mistaken, m'm, there's blood on it." He bent down and picked up the heavy branch.

"Blood?" Meredith's stomach took a nasty turn. She glanced up again at the tree. "Oh, my. I wonder if Miss Duncan was under the tree when Tom sawed off the branch. The blow could have sent her into the rockery."

"Could have happened that way." Reggie's voice sounded strange. "What I'm wondering, Mrs. Llewellyn, is why he didn't say nothing about it. He must have seen her fall. Seems very strange to me that he'd leave her out here all night without saying nothing 'til this morning."

Meredith had to agree. She remembered Tom's face earlier when he'd tried to tell her he'd found Kathleen's body. His shock and distress had been genuine. She felt quite certain of that.

"I suppose it could have been Davie," Reggie said. "After all, he's a bit of a sissy, ain't he. Wouldn't say boo to a goose, that one. Maybe Tom sent him to saw off the branch and when it hit Miss Duncan he got too scared to say nothing."

Meredith stared at him in dismay. Davie Gray was the assistant Tom had recently hired to help him with the heavy work. She'd noticed that the lad seemed a little quiet and shy, but Tom seemed satisfied with his labor. She hated to think Davie could be responsible for such a dreadful accident.

"I don't think Tom would have allowed him to prune a tree," she said, more to convince herself than Reggie. "Tom's very protective of them. I'm quite sure he would have taken care of that himself."

Reggie's skeptical expression did nothing to ease her concern. "Reckon the best thing we can do is to ask Tom about it."

"I shall do so, just as soon as I've addressed the pupils." She grasped her skirt to raise the hem an inch. "I'd like you to stay here with Miss Duncan until the doctor arrives. I'd like to make sure no one else sees her like that."

"Yes, m'm." Reggie touched his forehead with his fingers. "I'll see to it, don't you worry."

Worry, Meredith thought, as she hurried across the lawn to the school. How could she not worry, when someone was responsible for the death of a beloved teacher?

How could she possibly explain that to the young women waiting for her in assembly? What would they all do without Kathleen's efficient contribution to their education?

This was a black day for Bellehaven, indeed.

As if to emphasize her thoughts, a dark cloud drifted across the sun, sending a wide shadow across the grass. At the same moment, a wisp of white seemed to float by the corner of the building, only to vanish in the next second.

"I don't know what's going on." Olivia Bunting paused on the stairs to push her cap back up from her eyebrows, then picked up her mop and bucket again. "All I know is that someone called a general assembly and that's where they all went."

Trailing up the stairs behind her, Grace Parker winced as the carpet sweeper she carried banged against her ankles. "They never call for an assembly on a Sunday unless it's something really important. The last time was when one of the debs painted 'Votes for Women' all over the music room walls."

Olivia's snort of disgust echoed down the curving staircase. "Don't know why they'd get in a tizzy over that. Them teachers are all on the side of the suffragettes."

"Yeah, but they're not supposed to be, are they." Reaching the top of the stairs, Grace dumped the sweeper onto the narrow strip of carpet. "Young ladies are supposed to act proper at all times. Painting words on walls is not proper."

"If you ask me, there's a lot going on around here that's not proper."

"Like what?"

Olivia shrugged. "Not me place to spread gossip, is it."

Sensing a scandal behind her friend's words, Grace gave her a hefty nudge in the ribs with her elbow. "Come on. You know you're dying to tell me."

Olivia glanced down the long corridor. "All right. But don't tell no one. I don't want to get her in trouble."

Grace caught her breath. "Get who in trouble?"

"Well, that's just it. I don't know exactly who she was, but I do know it were one of them debs. I saw her sneaking through the door after lights out. I reckon she were meeting a man out there."

"Oo, 'eck." A delicious shiver raced down Grace's back. "Did you see him?"

"Course not, silly." Olivia started down the hallway. "If Mona caught me mucking about outside she'd box me ears."

Grace pinched her lips together as she began pushing the sweeper back and forth. She didn't like Monica Fingle one little bit. It was no wonder everyone called her Mona behind her back. The wretched housekeeper moaned about everything.

She shoved the sweeper ahead of her with vicious little jabs. If she was housekeeper in a big house she'd treat the maids a whole lot better than Mona treated her and Olivia. That she would.

Grace glanced down to the end of the hallway. Olivia had just started sloshing a wet rag over the windows. One day, Grace vowed, she'd find someone to marry her, and then she wouldn't have to be a housemaid no more. She'd be a lady, like them debs all lined up in the assembly hall. Then she'd tell Mona exactly what she thought of her. That she would.

The spacious assembly hall had once served as a ballroom when the mansion was occupied by Lord Davenport and his wife. When Stuart Hamilton bought the sprawling building he had the room renovated, removing the plaster cherubs and grapevines that had adorned the walls before adding a stage and lectern.

The glittering crystal chandeliers and the pale blue carpeting on the stairs leading to the balcony were all that remained of the room's once magnificent splendor. Now fifty young women sat and waited in restless anticipation for their headmistress's announcement.

Voices buzzed in discreet conversation when Meredith entered the hall. Felicity and Essie sat on the platform, with Kathleen's empty chair between them, as if guarding the space that would never again be occupied.

Essie's blotchy complexion must have served as a warning of a serious situation, since the ripple of murmurs died away the minute Meredith walked out to the middle of the stage.

She paused, waiting for complete quiet to settle over the upturned faces. Deciding not to beat about the bush, she filled her lungs with air. "I regret to inform you all that Miss Duncan has passed away quite suddenly this morning."

Again she paused as shocked cries and quiet weeping erupted from the audience in front of her. After a moment or two she raised her hand. When only a single sob or two interrupted the silence, she continued.

"Let us all take a minute to bow our heads in respect for our dear departed." When a suitable interval had passed, she looked up. "Home management classes will be suspended until a suitable replacement is found. Meanwhile, I would like all of you to confine yourselves to your rooms until mealtime, in order to observe this grievous tragedy."

A murmur ran through her audience. Again she waited for quiet. "Thank you. You are dismissed."

Watching the girls solemnly file out, she heard Essie weeping behind her. The young teacher's chin drooped, and her frail body shook with sobs.

With a rare show of sympathy, Felicity draped an arm around Essie's trembling shoulders. "Chin up, old fruit. Kathleen wouldn't want you to collapse on her behalf. She'd expect you to keep a stiff upper lip for the sake of the girls."

Essie struggled to stifle her sobs with a lace-edged handkerchief. "She looked so awful, just lying there. I . . . keep thinking how . . . dreadful it must have been to die all alone wi-without anyone to comfort her."

The last word had ended on a wail, and Felicity clicked her tongue. "Pull yourself together, Essie. You must take charge of your emotions. You know very well we can't let our pupils see you like this."

Meredith was about to speak when a male voice interrupted her. "I have a powder here that will help calm her."

She turned to face the sturdy figure standing a few feet away. "Dr. Mitchell. Thank goodness." She crossed the stage and hurried down the steps to join him. "I'm afraid Essie is terribly upset, as are we all."

"So I imagine." He set his black bag down on the nearest chair and opened it.

The first time Meredith had met Ian Mitchell, he'd

seemed far too young to be a licensed physician. She'd been surprised to learn later that he'd arrived in the world five years before her.

With his dark hair curling on his forehead, a trim figure in spite of his hardy build, and brown eyes that twinkled as if sharing a delicious secret, he projected a youthfulness that was both pleasing and somewhat disconcerting to his patients.

Those eyes regarded Meredith now with grave concern. "What happened to Miss Duncan?"

"We don't really know." She took the small white packet he handed her. "I thought she might have tripped and hit her head, but then Reggie saw the branch and it had blood on it, and I'm afraid—" She broke off when she saw the doctor's startled expression. "Let me just give this to Felicity and I'll take you to see Kathleen."

It took her only a moment or two to deliver the packet and extract a promise from Felicity that she would stay with Essie until the distressed teacher felt more composed. Then Meredith rejoined the doctor and led him out of the hall.

Dr. Mitchell waited until they were outside the building before asking, "What's all this about blood on a branch?"

"I'll show you." Lifting her skirts, she headed toward the rockery, with the doctor hot on her heels.

Reggie was pacing back and forth when they reached him. "I have to get back to me burst pipe," he told Meredith as soon as she was within earshot. "If I don't get it fixed, I'll have a bloomin' mess all over the floor."

"I'm going to need someone to help me remove the body." Dr. Mitchell paused by the still figure beneath the blanket. "I'd appreciate it if you could give me a hand."

"All right, but make it quick." Reggie actually shivered.

"Sitting here with her gave me the willies." He jerked his head at the rockery.

For a fleeting moment Meredith wondered if Reggie had seen what she'd seen—the strange phenomenon of wispy clouds floating around on the ground. In the next instant she chided herself for paying attention to her silly illusions. She needed to heed Felicity's words and collect herself. One distraught teacher was quite enough.

"Thank you, Reggie," she said, trying not to flinch as the doctor strode to the rockery and pulled back the blanket.

He spent some time moving Kathleen's head from side to side, until Meredith could watch no longer. She stared into the trees instead, watching the sunlight dance through the branches and create paint-dappled patterns of light across the path.

Just as she was about to turn away, she saw it again—a puff of cloud close to the ground, weaving in and out of the trees. As she stared, the cloud seemed to take form, evolving into the willowy shape of a woman with long hair floating behind her. One transparent hand lifted and appeared to beckon to her.

Meredith's sharp exclamation turned both men's heads.

Dr. Mitchell was the first to speak. He stood, wiping his hands on the small white towel he'd produced from his bag. "What is it, Mrs. Llewellyn? Is something wrong?"

Reggie just stared into the trees, following Meredith's gaze. "I can't see nothing."

Meredith lifted a shaking hand to point. "There," she whispered. "Right over there."

She turned toward the men, aggravated by their blank expressions as they peered at the spot.

Unable to believe they couldn't see what she saw, she

switched her gaze back to the trees. The apparition had vanished.

"It was there," she said, her voice trembling. "I saw it. First it looked like a cloud, but then I saw it was a woman." Aware of how utterly ridiculous that sounded, she added weakly, "At least, it appeared to be a woman. She seemed to be looking right at me."

Dr. Mitchell dropped the towel in his bag without comment, though Reggie gave her a sympathetic look. "Probably one of the girls having a game with you," he said.

"If that is so, it's in remarkably bad taste." The doctor reached into his bag. "More likely it's a result of the shock." He handed another small packet to Meredith. "Take this and lie down for an hour or so. You'll feel much better after a rest."

Meredith took the packet and slipped it into her pocket. Somehow she doubted a rest would banish the strange things happening to her mind.

"Now let me take a look at that branch." Dr. Mitchell moved over to where the branch lay. "Is this the one?"

"Yeah," Reggie answered. "I noticed there was blood all over it."

The doctor picked up the bulky limb. After a moment or two he lowered it back to the ground. "There's no question that's blood on there. I'm afraid I shall have to call in the constable."

Meredith uttered a cry of dismay. "Is that really necessary? It would be so upsetting for the girls. Couldn't you possibly report it as an unfortunate accident and leave it at that?"

"I'm afraid not." The doctor's expression worried her. "It appears that the blow from the branch was responsible for Miss Duncan's demise. I'm afraid, however, that it was hardly an accident."

"But . . ." Meredith glanced up at the tree. "Perhaps Miss Duncan happened to be passing under the tree when Tom sawed it off. In the twilight he might not have seen her. I think we should talk to him before taking up the constable's valuable time."

"By all means question your gardener." The doctor closed the clasp of his bag and stood. "But Miss Duncan did not die from a falling branch. She was struck with it."

Meredith stared at him, while Reggie gasped. "How'd you know that?" he demanded.

"Because," Dr. Mitchell said quietly, "the blow came from behind and low on the head. A falling branch would not have struck in that area with that much force. The blow was quite deliberate. In fact, I'm reasonably certain we are dealing with a murder."

Chapter 3

Mrs. Wilkins wiped her hands on her apron, leaving a smear of powdery flour. A bowl of shelled eggs stood in front of her on the kitchen table, waiting to be beaten. She picked up the whisk, reluctant to start whipping the mixture for fear she'd miss the whispered conversation between the two maids.

Olivia and Grace stood at the sink, supposedly peeling potatoes, though judging from the slow motion of their hands a large proportion of the vegetables still wore their skins.

Olivia's dark head leaned close to Grace's fair one, and the cook could tell the two of them were up to no good. Picking up the bowl of eggs, she edged around the table until she could hear Olivia's muttered words.

"I'm going to Witcheston, no matter what."

Grace gave her a fierce shake of her head. "It's not your day off. You'll get into trouble. You know what Mona's like. She could give you the sack."

"She won't know. Not unless you tell her." Olivia started peeling again. "You're not going to tell her, are you."

Again Grace shook her head. "You don't have to worry about me. But what if she asks?"

"Say you don't know."

"What if you get into trouble while you're there? You know them suffragettes are always getting arrested. What if you get caught and thrown in the clink?"

"Then you'll be serving dinner without me, won't you." Olivia paused, her dark eyes on her friend's face. "Unless you come with me."

Grace uttered a soft squeak, and Mrs. Wilkins could stand it no longer. "No," she said sharply. "She's not going with you. Neither of you are going anywhere, so there."

Olivia gave her an impudent toss of her head. "Says who?"

"Says me." Mrs. Wilkins put down the whisk and folded her arms across her chest. "I'll tell Miss Fingle, that's what I'll do."

"Telltale," Olivia muttered.

Mrs. Wilkins did not like being at odds with the maids. She had three daughters of her own, quite a bit older than Olivia and Grace, of course. All of her girls lived in London, and she hardly ever saw them. The maids helped ease the ache of missing her daughters. Even when they misbehaved, like right now. "Why don't you wait for your afternoon off," she suggested. "You can go to Witcheston and be back in time for supper."

Olivia threw the knife down and turned to face her. "I'm going tomorrow because the suffragettes are holding a big protest and I want to help them, that's why."

Mrs. Wilkins glanced at Grace, whose wide blue gaze

seemed fixed on Olivia's face. The cook could tell the child was torn between obeying the rules and supporting her friend. "You're not yet eighteen. The suffragettes know better than to let you protest with them."

"They won't know, will they." Olivia nudged Grace in the ribs. "We both look older when we're dressed up."

Now Mrs. Wilkins felt really worried. There was no stopping Olivia once she'd made up her mind. "Grace is right. If you get caught you could end up in prison." She leaned closer to the girls and lowered her voice to an ominous tone. "You know what they do to suffragettes in prison?"

Grace looked terrified, but Olivia merely shrugged. "They only beat you if you don't behave."

"They do worse than that," Mrs. Wilkins assured her, hoping Olivia wouldn't ask her what she meant by that. She knew that dreadful things happened to the protestors while they were locked up, but she didn't know any of the details and she didn't want to know.

"Well, then, we just won't have to get caught, that's all." Olivia's expression dared Grace to oppose her. "You coming with me or not?"

Grace sent a frightened glance at the cook, then whispered, "I s'pose so."

"That's that, then." Olivia fished in the cold water for her knife and picked up another potato.

Mrs. Wilkins pinched her lips together. She didn't like tattling on the girls. For the life of her she didn't. She liked being on good terms with them, sharing a laugh or two at Monica Fingle's expense. After all, if you couldn't laugh now and then, the world would be a pretty miserable place.

Not that she'd ever seen Monica laugh, or even smile come to that. Something must have happened to that woman to make her so shrewish. Mrs. Wilkins could even feel sorry for Monica when she didn't take out her bad temper on the girls. Always on their backs she was, telling them off for every little thing.

The cook picked up the whisk and started beating the eggs with a furious whirling of her wrist. She had a real problem on her hands now. If she said nothing and let the maids go to Witcheston and they got caught and thrown in jail, then she'd feel responsible for getting them into trouble. On the other hand, if she told Monica what the girls had planned, the housekeeper would come down on them like a felled oak. Mrs. Wilkins let out a long sigh. They'd probably end up not speaking to her and take weeks to forgive her.

She could hear the girls whispering again behind her, but she had no heart to listen. She knew what she had to do, and she didn't like it one bit.

Police Constable Cyril Shipham arrived shortly after noon. Having ridden his bicycle from the village under the hot sun, sweat bathed his forehead beneath the brim of his heavy helmet. He paused at the gates of Bellehaven to wipe his face with his handkerchief before tugging on the bell rope to announce his presence.

The long wait that followed did nothing to improve his temper. If there was one thing he couldn't abide, it was being kept waiting. By women, no less.

Cyril had no time for women. The harridan he'd been stupid enough to marry had cured him of any delusions he might have had about females. Nag, nag, nag from morning 'til night. Enough to drive a man insane.

His mother had been the same way. Never kept to a word or two when a dozen or more would do. She could make a whole story out of one tiny little mistake. Blimey, everything he did as a kid was a mistake in her eyes.

Thinking about his mother only intensified his frustration. He took it out on the bell rope, sending the harsh clang echoing across the wide lawn.

It was Tom's job to open the gate to visitors, providing they appeared to have good reason to visit the school. Meredith often had reservations about leaving such an important task in the elderly gardener's hands. He seemed to handle his duties efficiently enough, however, and since the bell could not always be heard from within the school building, it seemed prudent to let the arrangement stand.

As it was, she had not heard the impatient summons at the gate, and first learned of the constable's presence when he arrived at the door of her office.

"I expected to see Dr. Mitchell waiting for me," P.C. Shipham announced, rudely ignoring her polite greeting.

Well accustomed to the constable's open disapproval of Bellehaven and everyone connected to it, Meredith did her best to ignore the slight. "The doctor is waiting by Kath . . . by the body," she said, rising to her feet. "He was concerned that the area might be disturbed if he didn't keep watch over it until you arrived."

"Quite, quite." Shipham rather belatedly removed his helmet and tucked it under his arm. "Where is he then?"

"I'll be happy to take you there."

She began to move out from behind her desk, but he halted her with an imperious wave of his hand. "Just tell me where he is. I don't need no escort."

"I prefer to be there when you make your examination." Steeling herself against the constable's angry scowl, she brushed past him and marched to the door. "This way, please."

"I don't like meddling women nosing around when I'm investigating a crime."

Meredith tugged the door open. "As headmistress of this institution, I am entitled to all the facts regarding this tragic situation. I hardly categorize that as mere prying. If you prefer, I can call in the inspector, and we'll hold off your investigation until he arrives."

As she expected, the constable immediately changed his tune. "No need to call in the inspector. If you insist, I suppose I shall have to put up with it. Just stay out of my way while I do my duty."

"With pleasure," Meredith murmured.

She didn't speak again until they had reached Dr. Mitchell, who still sat on a rock, scribbling in a fat notebook. He jumped up as soon as he caught sight of them, relief flooding his face. "Thank heavens. I was beginning to think I'd be here all afternoon. I have surgery at two o'clock." He pulled a pocket watch from his vest pocket and gave it a harried glance. "Good Lord, is that the time?"

"All right, all right, keep your hair on," Shipham muttered. "Let me take a look here, then."

Once more Meredith had to avert her gaze as the constable poked and prodded around the spot where Kathleen lay. She wished heartily that the process was over, so that her dear friend could be laid to rest in the proper manner.

Concentrating her gaze on the thicket of trees, she found herself watching for a wisp of white cloud among the shadowy foliage. After several moments of seeing nothing but fronds of lacy ferns bowing in the gentle breeze, she felt assured that her momentary delusions had vanished.

P.C. Shipham invaded her thoughts with his brusque words. "All right, I've seen enough. Looks like she was clobbered with this branch, all right. Most likely that vagrant what's been hanging around the village lately."

Meredith swung around to face him. "Vagrant?"

Cyril ignored her and addressed Dr. Mitchell, instead. "Been into a lot of trouble he has. I was only telling the inspector the other day that I wouldn't be surprised if someone didn't end up getting hurt. I reckon he was looking for mischief when he came across her." He nodded at the lifeless form under the blanket. "That's what a woman gets for walking around on her own out here at night." He shook his head. "Should've known better, shouldn't she."

Meredith felt a strong urge to slap that self-satisfied smirk right off his face. "I'd like to know how a vagrant managed to get in here with the gates locked."

Shipham threw her a scathing glance. "Maybe they weren't locked. Maybe someone forgot to lock them. After all, you've got plenty of addle-headed females here that could easily forget something like that."

Meredith drew herself up to her full height. "I can assure you, Constable, that none of our young ladies are that irresponsible. In any case, Tom makes the rounds after lights out to assure that the gates are locked."

"Well, maybe he forgot. Not exactly swift on the uptake, is he."

Incensed, Meredith turned to the doctor for help. To her dismay he merely lifted his hands in a gesture of defeat.

"Well, that's that then." The constable snapped his notebook shut and shoved it in his breast pocket. "Reckon I'll be getting along. I take it you can handle that?" He nodded at Kathleen's dead body.

Compelled to pursue the matter, Meredith stepped closer to the constable. "What do you intend to do about this, then?"

Shipham shrugged and turned away. "Not much to do, I reckon. That there vagrant will be miles away by now."

"In other words, you are simply dismissing the whole thing without even investigating the possibility that a killer could still be lurking nearby and could very well present a danger to the young women in this school?"

His sneer convinced her she was wasting her breath. "There's no evidence to suggest he's still around. She were just in the wrong place at the wrong time, that's all. Happens a lot." Once more he addressed the doctor. "I'll make out a report of wrongful death by a person or persons unknown. That should take care of it. Good day to you, Doctor." With the briefest of nods in Meredith's direction he ambled off toward the gate.

Her indignation culminated in an explosion of wrath. "Dratted fool. Had it been a man lying there instead of a mere woman, that imbecile would have combed the grounds for evidence."

"Hush." Ian Mitchell raised a warning finger, his gaze on the retreating back of the constable. "He's barely out of earshot."

Heedless of his caution, she raged on. "It is men like that who drive women to ravage golf courses and break the windows of the pompous, bourgeois clubs men guard so fervently against female intrusion. Heaven preserve us from all such ignorant bigots."

The doctor shook his head. "I'm so sorry, Mrs. Llewellyn. I understand your frustration. Unfortunately, I don't see that there's much we can do about it."

"We shall see about that." Meredith sent another scowl after the constable. "If that numskull refuses to investigate the matter, then it falls upon me and my associates to do so. One way or another, we shall unearth the malicious wretch who did this to Kathleen and we shall see that he receives his just desserts."

"Mrs. Llewellyn—"

Still seething with resentment, Meredith turned on him. "Oh, for heaven's sake, Ian. Do call me Meredith. At least when we are out of earshot of the pupils. Surely we have known each other long enough to dispense with such tiresome proprieties?"

The doctor's cheeks grew warm. "Well, I suppose I could—"

"Besides." Meredith took one last long look at Kathleen's still figure beneath the blanket. "You're pronouncing it all wrong."

"I do beg your pardon." Ian's eyebrows rose. "Good Lord, why didn't you say something before?"

Meredith shrugged. "It really didn't irritate me until now. I'm sorry. I'm not in the best of moods. I'd better find Reggie to help you with Kathleen."

"I'd appreciate that."

She nodded and turned away, then paused when he added, "Mrs. Llewell—Meredith. A word of warning. Whoever did this could be extremely dangerous. If you try to investigate, you could be taking a grave risk with your life. Moreover, Constable Shipham will not take kindly to you meddling in a situation that he considers resolved. I suggest you think twice before treading on his territory."

"I appreciate your concern, but I will not rest until I know that someone has paid for Kathleen's death." She smiled at him. "I promise I shall watch where I tread."

"I wish I could assist you." The doctor shook his head. "Because of my position, however, I must refrain from taking any part in such a controversial pursuit."

"I understand." She glanced one last time at her friend.

"Please take care of her for me." She hurried away, before the prickling under her lids could turn once more to tears.

Instead of crossing the lawn, she chose to take the path through the gardens. She needed time to catch her breath— to decide what her first step should be. A good place to start would be to question anyone who might have seen Kathleen wandering around the night before.

Upon reaching the flower beds, she paused, her heart aching as she wondered who would create such a profusion of color and beauty now that Kathleen had gone. Tom would tend to the flowers with his usual care, but it had been Kathleen who had chosen the plants and designed their arrangement in the beds. The teacher would be missed on so many levels.

In spite of the sun's rays warming her back, Meredith shivered as a chill breeze touched her cheek. Conscious of someone watching her, she spun around. Her imagination was playing tricks on her again. She was quite alone.

She turned back to the flowers, intent on picking some for the foyer. She had actually reached out when a slight movement from across the beds stilled her hand. Straightening, she stared at a spot a few feet away at the edge of the path.

The patch of mist swirled like a veil caught in the wind. It seemed to ebb and flow around the figure of a woman, hiding her from sight one minute and allowing a tantalizing glimpse of her the next.

Meredith shut her eyes tight. She should have taken the powder Ian had given her. "Go away," she muttered. "You are a figment of my imagination. Be off with you."

Only the fluttering of leaves overhead answered her. Cautiously she opened one eye, then opened them both wide. The apparition still floated in front of her.

Every instinct urged Meredith to turn tail and run as fast as she could back to the safety of the school hallways. Her fear, however, held her fast to the spot.

The wisp of gray mist hovered above the path, with just a faint shadow of a figure in its midst. Although she couldn't see it clearly, Meredith felt a strange sense of desperation emitting from the weaving cloud.

Her lips stiff with fright, she whispered, "Who are you? What do you want?"

The figure immediately became brighter, more distinct. The woman's hair flowed about her shoulders, and she raised a graceful hand and pointed at Meredith's feet.

Heart pounding, Meredith looked down, but could see nothing but the toes of her shoes peeking out from beneath the hem of her skirt. When she raised her head again, the mist had vanished.

Shaken to the core, she fought to regain her breath. In that brief instant, she had recognized the apparition. As ridiculous as it might seem, she had no doubts at all. The image was the ghost of Kathleen Duncan.

Chapter 4

Mrs. Wilkins tapped gingerly on the door of Monica Fingle's office. She wasn't happy with herself at all, but she felt strongly that it was her duty to protect the maids, even if they got cross with her for it.

Monica's thin voice called out from the other side of the door. "Enter!"

Mrs. Wilkins entered.

As always, she felt intimidated by Monica's presence. The housekeeper sat in her chair as if she had a board strapped to her back. The hollows under her cheekbones were deep enough to hoard acorns and her jagged teeth stuck out over her bottom lip when she smiled. Which, mercifully, wasn't often, thanks to the white lace ruff she always wore with her black dresses, which limited movement of her chin.

"I'm surprised you have the time to pay me a visit," Monica said, with a meaningful glance at the large clock on the wall. "Aren't you supposed to be in the kitchen attending to the midday meal?"

Having put off her visit to the housekeeper for as long as possible, Mrs. Wilkins felt affronted by this rebuke. "Dinner has already been served," she said, sharpening her tone just a little. "The maids are washing the dishes in the kitchen, and I have more than enough time to spare before getting the supper ready."

Monica sighed and laid her pen down on the blotter. "Very well. What is it?"

For a second or two Mrs. Wilkins wavered. Then she remembered the vague hints she'd heard about the suffragettes and the appalling treatment they received in prison. "It's the maids," she said, speaking quickly before she lost her nerve again. "They're talking about going to Witcheston to join in the protest with the suffragettes tomorrow. I told them it was dangerous but they won't listen to me and—"

Monica's black eyes gleamed. "Are you telling me they intend to take unscheduled time off?"

"Yes, Miss Fingle."

"Together?"

"I'm afraid so."

"That is quite unacceptable. The maids each have an afternoon off every week. One on Wednesday and one on Thursday, do they not?"

"Yes, Miss Fingle." Mrs. Wilkins was beginning to wish she'd kept her mouth shut and let the girls take their chances with the suffragettes.

"Tomorrow is Monday." Monica waited, as if expecting an answer to the obvious statement.

The cook reluctantly obliged. "Yes, Miss Fingle."

"In any case, we cannot have them going off together.

Either they take their allotted time off, or they do without. Is that clear?"

"Yes, Miss Fingle." The cook hesitated, then added cautiously, "Will you be telling them that, then?"

Monica's thin eyebrows drew together. "Isn't that your responsibility?"

Mrs. Wilkins started twisting an apron string around her fingers. "Well, yes, it is, but—"

"Well, then, see to it." Monica picked up her pen as a signal the conversation was at an end.

Mrs. Wilkins pursed her lips. "Yes, Miss Fingle."

She was about to turn away when Monica said quietly, "One more thing. It is my duty to inform you that Miss Duncan has met with an unfortunate accident and has passed away."

Frozen to the spot, Mrs. Wilkins tried to make sense of the preposterous words. "Passed away?"

"Yes. You may inform the rest of the staff at your discretion."

"Miss Duncan is *dead*?" Even saying it out loud didn't make it any more believable.

"I believe that is what is meant by passed away, yes." Without looking up, Monica waved her pen at the door.

Stiff with shock, Mrs. Wilkins turned back toward the door. Just as she reached it, Monica added, "I shall hold you responsible, Mrs. Wilkins, if those girls should ignore your orders. We can't allow that sort of disobedience in this establishment. It would set a very bad example for our pupils. I expect you to have complete control over your underlings. Don't disappoint me."

"Yes, Miss Fingle. I mean, no, Miss Fingle. I'll do my best."

Mrs. Wilkins shut the door with a quiet snap, though she

felt more inclined to slam it. What a cold fish that Monica was to be so concerned about the maids when a good woman like Miss Duncan lay dead.

Even now she couldn't believe it. Muttering to herself, she hurried back down to the kitchen. She'd have to tell the girls, but she doubted very much that, or anything, would stop them from going to Witcheston, short of imprisoning them somewhere, and that was highly unlikely.

She'd do her best, as she'd promised, of course, but if Olivia and Grace had made up their minds, there wasn't much she could do about it, except hope with all her might that Monica never found out about it. And that, she had to admit, was just as unlikely.

"I tell you I saw Kathleen's ghost!" In her agitation, Meredith flung out her hand, causing a vase of carefully arranged roses to topple.

Felicity dived forward, and with remarkable agility caught the vase before it fell to the carpet. She set it down again and wiped her wet fingers on her skirt. "Meredith, dear, I know you're upset but . . . really. A ghost?"

Meredith sank onto the nearest armchair. Normally the teachers' lounge provided rare moments of peace in the hubbub generally experienced within the walls of Belle-haven. She felt no such calming effects this day, however. Even the tasteful pink flowered wallpaper and rose carpet, usually so pleasing to the eye, failed to settle her jostling nerves. "I knew you wouldn't believe me," she muttered.

Essie came forward and laid a hand on her shoulder. The petite woman's puffy eyes still bore the signs of her weeping, and her blotchy cheeks made her look even younger than usual as she peered anxiously into Meredith's face. "It's unlike you to lose composure this way, Meredith. You are always so strong and sensible."

Meredith summoned a weak smile. "I don't feel very sensible right now. I know what I saw. I also know how impossible it sounds, but I think Kathleen needs something from me."

Felicity flung herself onto the davenport, causing a maroon silk cushion to bounce off onto the floor. Her voice sounded muffled as she bent over to pick it up. "Needs what?"

"I don't know. I didn't wait around to find out. But it must be important."

Felicity straightened. "Meredith, you really must get this ridiculous notion out of your head. Ghosts don't haunt flower beds in the middle of the day. They haunt houses. At night. What's important is what the constable is doing about Kathleen's murder. I trust he's looking into it?"

"I'm afraid not." Meredith recounted her conversation with PC Shipham. Felicity snorted throughout, while Essie uttered little gasps of dismay.

"Typical," Felicity muttered, when Meredith reached the end of her account. "What did you expect from the man? Absolutely relishes his power over women, and doesn't care one little bit what happened as long as it doesn't inconvenience him."

"I expected him to hunt down the perpetrator of this horrible crime and put him behind bars." Meredith sighed. "At least I'd hoped that's what he'd do."

"Well, I can see why you're upset." Felicity fluffed up the cushion and shoved it behind her back. "No wonder you're imagining ghosts. Did you take the powder Dr. Mitchell gave you?"

Deciding to ignore that question, Meredith stood. "I

want you both to come with me now, to the gardens. I'm hoping you'll see what I saw—what I keep seeing—and maybe then you will believe what I believe."

Essie shook her head. "Oh, no, I couldn't. A ghost . . . I mean . . . I just couldn't."

"Of course you can." Felicity rose to her feet. "In any case, there's nothing to see. But if it will make Meredith feel better, we should go with her." She glanced at the grandfather clock ticking methodically in the corner of the room. "We have time before the afternoon sessions."

She strode to the door and looked back at the two of them. "Well, are you coming? Let's get this over with."

Meredith looked at Essie, who seemed rooted to the spot. "I promise you, Essie, Kathleen is not at all threatening. In fact, she looks almost tranquil, considering what's at stake."

Essie whimpered again. "I'd much rather you went without me."

"Don't be such a baby." Felicity scowled across the room. "We all know there's no such thing as ghosts. What Meredith saw was probably a patch of mist, that's all. Happens often in a waning summer. When one's in shock, it's not all that unusual to imagine things that aren't there."

Meredith took hold of Essie's arm and gently pulled her toward the door. "I need you there," she said, before they followed Felicity out into the hallway. "Felicity has already made up her mind and Kathleen might not show herself to her. You, however, are more sympathetic, and I'm hoping you will see Kathleen as I did."

"I don't want to see her," Essie mumbled, but nevertheless she allowed herself to be led outside and along the path to the gardens.

Felicity arrived ahead of them, and stood among the

flowers, both hands planted on her hips. "All right," she said, as Meredith and Essie reached her, "now show us the ghost."

"I saw it right there." Meredith pointed toward the edge of the path. "She only appeared clearly for a second or two, but I recognized Kathleen right away."

"What was she wearing?"

Meredith struggled to remember. "Some sort of filmy gown, I think. Why?"

"Because it was most likely one of the girls playing a trick on you, that's why. And when I find out who it was, she will pay dearly for her impertinent behavior."

Meredith thinned her mouth. "Let us all stand still and be quiet, please. Kathleen is not likely to appear while we are squabbling about this."

Felicity grunted, but refrained from answering.

Not that Meredith could blame her skepticism. Even as she had spoken the words, she had to acknowledge how foolish she sounded. It would be so much simpler to dismiss the entire episode as a mere symptom of her distress over Kathleen's sudden demise.

Yet, if she had really seen a ghost, how could she turn her back on her friend when she needed her badly enough to reach out to her from the grave?

Then again, since Kathleen had not yet been buried, she wasn't in her grave. Perhaps, once the service had taken place and Kathleen was in her final resting place, she might find the peace to depart in the proper manner.

Holding her breath, Meredith waited as the silence seemed to envelop all three of them. Only a faint breeze stirring the leaves above their heads disturbed the uncanny stillness among the flower beds.

Essie pressed closer to Meredith, and she could feel the

younger woman trembling against her arm. Concentrating hard on the spot where she'd seen Kathleen earlier, Meredith willed her late friend to appear.

For several long moments the three of them stood motionless. Then, right above their heads, the branches fluttered, and a sparrow chirped loudly to its mate.

Essie jumped sharply and uttered a frightened squeal. The startled birds flew from the tree and flapped away.

Felicity turned and held out her hands in appeal. "How long are we supposed to stand here waiting for something that's never going to happen? Can't you just admit it was all in your imagination?"

Meredith sighed. "Maybe you're right. I'm sorry I brought you out here. Let's get back to the house and take care of our pupils."

"About time, too." Felicity stomped off, while Essie's small hand crept into the crook of Meredith's arm. "I'm sorry," she said, her voice subdued, "I know you really wanted to believe it."

"Yes, I did." Meredith patted the hand on her arm. "Silly of me, I suppose. Once Kathleen has a proper burial and is at peace, I'm sure I won't have any more of these foolish illusions."

She walked with Essie back down the path, trying to reconcile reality with what she was certain she'd seen earlier. Perhaps she had imagined the whole thing, after all. The events of that dreadful day had been traumatic enough to confuse anyone's mind.

It really didn't matter, however, whether or not Kathleen was coming back from the dead to give her a message. The important thing was to find out who had committed such a foul crime. She owed it to her late friend to see that justice was done.

Somehow she would ferret out the truth, with or without the help of her skeptical associates. And neither one of them could dissuade her from that path.

Mrs. Wilkins tackled the maids right after supper. She waited until the dishes had been washed and replaced in the cupboards, and everything in the kitchen was spick-and-span once more.

She could tell by the way Grace kept dropping things that she was nervous about the proposed scheme the next day. She hoped the girl's understandable apprehension might help her accept the argument that nothing but trouble awaited them in Witcheston.

She watched Olivia carry the clean milk churn to the door to await the milkman in the morning. That girl didn't have a nervous bone in her body. Always flirting with danger, she was, and dragging poor Grace in with her.

Mrs. Wilkins braced herself. Someone had to stop them, and it might as well be her. Even if they did get cross with her for interfering. "I had a word with Miss Fingle," she announced, as the girls prepared to leave. "She has absolutely forbidden you two to go to Witcheston tomorrow."

Grace uttered a cry of dismay, while Olivia swung around, her dark eyes blazing. "What'd you go and do that for?"

Mrs. Wilkins flinched, but met the furious gaze. "I did it because I'm worried you'll get yourselves in a whole lot of trouble, that's why. I don't want to see you both end up in prison. They beat suffragettes in prison, you know. And worse. Much worse."

Olivia tossed her head, dislodging her cap. She removed the pin, shoved the cap back in place, and jabbed the pin back in her hair. "We won't get caught, so we won't end up in prison. Both me and Gracie can run fast, can't we." She nudged her friend with her arm.

Mrs. Wilkins could tell Grace was fighting between her fear of being caught by the bobbies and her loyalty to her friend. Taking her silence for agreement, the cook put an arm about the young girl's thin shoulders. "See? Grace doesn't really want to go, do you, duck."

"Then I'll go by myself." Olivia twisted around and headed for the door.

"No, I'm going with you!" Grace pulled out of Mrs. Wilkins's grasp and ran after Olivia.

The door closed behind the two of them, and Mrs. Wilkins sank onto a chair, her head in her hands. She'd tried. She'd done the best she could. Now all she could do was sit and wait, and pray to the good Lord to bring those two foolish girls home safe and sound.

Confusing dreams disturbed Meredith's sleep that night, and she awoke with a headache. It was a struggle for her to get through her classes that morning, especially since the matter of replacing Kathleen weighed heavily on her mind.

Her students seemed to have recovered from the shock of Kathleen's death for the most part, though some remained abnormally subdued. They had been told that Kathleen's death was an accident, and Meredith prayed she could maintain the falsehood, at least until the person responsible had been apprehended.

All of the students were anxious to know what would happen to their home management studies and Meredith assured them a replacement would be found, though she seriously doubted she would find anyone as competent as her late friend had been, especially on short notice.

She felt a vast relief when at last the bell rang for the end of class. The pupils collected their paints and brushes, and leaving their landscapes on the easels to dry, filed out of the room.

Meredith was about to follow them when a tall figure filled the doorway, blocking her exit. Stuart Hamilton's grim expression told her at once that he'd heard of Kathleen's demise, and that he was far from pleased.

It wasn't often that she received a visit from the owner of Bellehaven, but on every occasion that they had met, Meredith had felt at a disadvantage for some strange reason.

Maybe it was his impressive height, his direct gaze from dark eyes that challenged her every word, or the commanding way in which he addressed her— as if she were one of the pupils instead of the headmistress.

Whichever it was, she constantly swayed between admiring his confident, forthright manner and hating his arrogance. She found herself dithering on more than one issue, and Meredith did not like to be distracted by anyone, much less a man who had no working knowledge of the effort it took to keep Bellehaven running smoothly.

As always, she had difficulty meeting his gaze and in an effort to avoid her usual confusion in his presence, she forestalled his greeting. "Mr. Hamilton. I presume you have heard the tragic news?"

"I have indeed." He stepped inside the room, somehow diminishing its space by his presence. "I came as soon as I heard."

Meredith turned away, hoping to collect her scattered thoughts. She wasn't sure just how much he knew about the circumstances of Kathleen's death, and she wasn't about to inform him of her own conjectures. "It is such a great loss. Apart from losing a good friend, we have lost a valuable instructress. It will be extremely difficult to replace Miss Duncan."

"Which is precisely why I am here." Stuart Hamilton moved over to an easel and peered at the painting resting on it. "Good Lord. What's that supposed to be?"

Meredith thinned her lips. She might be at liberty to criticize the work of her students, but how dare this man feel justified in doing so. "I will commence to search right away for a suitable replacement for Miss Duncan," she said primly. "I will be sure to inform you as soon as that has been accomplished."

"No need." Hamilton straightened, hooked a finger in his watch chain, and pulled the gold watch from his waistcoat pocket. After glancing at it, he moved toward the door. "I already have a replacement."

Stunned, Meredith stared at his broad back. "I beg your pardon?"

He swung around to face her, once more unsettling her. "Her name is Sylvia Montrose. She comes with the best recommendation, she's adequately qualified, trustworthy, and experienced."

"But—" In her agitation, Meredith took two steps toward him.

He raised a hand. "I'm quite sure you recognize that time is of the essence here. Miss Montrose will arrive early tomorrow. Should you disagree with my choice, after a suitable trial period, of course, we shall then discuss the matter further."

With that, he swept through the door, leaving Meredith astounded, disconcerted, and thoroughly offended.

Chapter 5

Having had the matter so abruptly taken out of her hands, Meredith was left with a few minutes to soothe her rattled nerves before joining the rest of the teachers in the lounge.

She decided to clear her head with a brisk walk in the midday sun, a pursuit she often enjoyed while sorting through problems in her head.

Despite her resolve to forget the strange illusions that had beset her of late, she found herself drawn against her will to the flower gardens. To her relief, she could see no vapors or mist hovering over the path when she arrived, a little breathless from hurrying across the lawns.

She took a moment or two to breathe in the glorious fragrance of the lavender. The sweet-smelling flowers had been Kathleen's favorite. She'd pick the tiny blossoms and dry them, then sew them into little silk pouches to lay in her chest of drawers.

Meredith still had two of the pouches Kathleen had given her, though the fragrance had long since dissipated. She would keep them forever now, she decided, as a memento of her dear departed friend.

Stooping down to the pale blue flowers, she plucked a stem or two and brought them to her nose. As she did so, a familiar chill wafted across her back. She knew, before she straightened, what she would see.

The strange mist swirled beneath the trees, just a few feet away. She could feel the cold emanating from the heart of the cloud, where the form of the woman wavered back and forth as if caught in a rippling tide of water.

The very last thing Meredith wanted to do was confront what she now felt certain had to be Kathleen's ghost. She could not ignore the fact, however, that her friend needed help of some kind. Gathering up her courage, she lifted her chin and faced the apparition.

After a quick glance around to make sure she was quite alone, she took a step closer. The cloud flowed backward, keeping the same distance. She halted, afraid it would disappear altogether.

Her heart beat forcefully in her chest, robbing her of air, and she had to force her lips to move. "Kathleen," she said, in little more than a whisper. "I know it's you. What do you want?"

Just for a moment, the face of the woman became distinct, and Kathleen's face looked back at her with strange, sightless eyes.

Meredith thought her heart would stop beating, but then it raced on as she stared at the ghost. "What do you want?" she repeated, a little more loudly this time.

The woman faded, her body swirling into nothing but mist. Sorely disappointed, Meredith was about to turn away when the apparition formed again. This time, Kathleen raised her arm and pointed at the flower beds.

Meredith followed the gesture and stared in confusion at the colorful blossoms. After a moment she noticed a few clumps of yellow petals in between the thriving plants. Dandelions. Kathleen had always been a stickler for keeping clean flower beds.

She turned back to the apparition, only to find it had disappeared. "I'll tell Tom," Meredith said, talking now to empty air. "Don't worry, Kathleen. I'll make sure Tom gets the beds weeded."

She waited a moment, but the air about her remained perfectly still. Sighing in frustration, she turned around, and received a nasty jolt when she realized she was not alone. Davie Gray, Tom's timid assistant, stood just a few feet away, an odd expression on his pallid face. She was about to speak to him when he turned and slunk off into the trees like a wounded animal.

Jogging along the road on the back of Farmer Brown's cart, Grace's teeth jarred against each other with every bump. It wasn't often she complained about Olivia's ideas, but this adventure was beginning to lose its enchantment before it had actually begun.

Olivia must have sensed her discomfort, as she leaned closer, raising her voice above the rattling of the cart and the clatter of hooves. "What's the matter? You look as if you've taken a bite out of a sour apple."

"I was just wishing you could have found a more comfortable way to get to Witcheston." Grace softened her criticism with a wry smile. "My backbone feels like it's coming apart."

Olivia shrugged. "It was either this or ride our bicycles into town. That would have taken us all day."

Grace gripped the wooden bars at her side and winced as a splinter dug into her palm. At the same moment one of the cart wheels bounced in and out of a rut, slamming her posterior up and down on the hard platform. "Ow!" She sent Olivia a reproachful look. "That hurt. And all these cauliflowers and cabbages really stink. And look at us, we're getting smothered in dust and dirt. We're going to look like ragamuffins by the time we get into town."

Olivia fidgeted from side to side, and Grace could tell her friend was as uncomfortable as she was. "Yeah, well," Olivia muttered, "we're suffragettes. We're supposed to suffer for the cause."

Grace's bruised bottom made her feel unusually resentful. "I just hope all this is worth it. I'd rather be scrubbing the kitchen floor than bumping around on this cart with all these smelly vegetables."

"Oh, stop whining." Olivia bit her lip as the cart bounced over yet another rut in the road. "We'll be there soon. You'll feel better once we're off this thing and we can join the suffragettes." Her frown vanished. "Just think, we're on our way to our very first protest. Don't you think that's really exciting?"

Right then, the only thing Grace could find remotely exciting was a warm bath to ease her tortured bones. Still, she was on her way now, and it was a bit late to admit that this wasn't one of Olivia's best ideas. "I suppose so," she said, taking a firmer grip on the bars. "I just hope we don't end up in prison, that's all."

Olivia shook her head. "You're such a wet blanket. I don't know why I asked you to come with me."

Grace would have vastly preferred that she hadn't been

asked, but she refrained from saying so. If she was to survive this day, she needed to stay in Olivia's good books. Otherwise she could very likely find herself abandoned on the streets of Witcheston.

It occurred to her then to wonder how on earth the two of them would get back to Bellehaven. It was unlikely the farmer would stay in town once he had deposited his load of vegetables at the market.

Olivia hadn't mentioned as yet how she'd planned to return. Grace pondered the problem for a moment or two, then decided to put it out of her mind for now. She had far too much to worry about for the next few hours.

By the time the farmer pulled up in Witcheston's market square, Grace would have walked through fire to get off that cart. Even Olivia appeared to be limping as they crossed the busy street to the corner, where a group of musicians played a lively tune on an assortment of instruments.

Grace stared about her, anxious to take in all the unfamiliar sights and sounds. She'd only been into town three times before this, when she was a child. This was her first grown-up visit, and if she hadn't been so nervous about the protest, she'd have thoroughly enjoyed the experience.

The huge windows of the department store with their dazzling array of beautiful clothes, furniture, and a breathtaking selection of china and glass fascinated her beyond description. She could have spent the entire day simply staring at all the wonders.

Olivia, however, tugged her arm, urging her to hurry. "We have to get to the town hall," she said, panting as they sped in and out of the pedestrians on the street. "The protest is supposed to start at midday."

As if to mock her words, a church bell nearby started chiming. "That's twelve o'clock," Olivia cried, and dashed across the road, startling a black horse pulling a fancy carriage.

The horse reared up, and the driver angrily shouted as he struggled to rein in the agitated animal. A young man passing by stepped out and grabbed the reins, calming the horse until it stood still.

Grace stared at the gentleman in admiration, thinking how brave of him and how gallant. When she looked across the street, Olivia had disappeared.

A nasty cold feeling struck her in the chest. She had no idea where the town hall was or how to get to it. Gingerly she stepped out into the road and crossed to the other side unscathed.

To her huge relief, Olivia stood at the next corner, beckoning furiously. Hurrying toward her, Grace vowed not to let her friend out of her sight again.

"Wait," Olivia said, as Grace reached her. "Look over there."

Grace followed Olivia's nod, expecting to see a group of suffragettes. Instead, all she saw of interest was a young girl with shiny dark brown hair arguing with a much older man.

"Where are—" she started to ask, but Olivia interrupted her.

"That's one of the girls from the school." She stared across the street at the arguing couple. "I don't believe it. You know who that is she's talking to?"

Grace peered at the stout man standing over the young girl. "He looks familiar, but—"

Olivia prodded her in the side. "That's Victor Silkwood, that's who. You know. The bloke that owns all that land and that big posh house. I wonder what that girl is doing talking to him like that."

"Perhaps she's his daughter."

"No, she's not. He only has sons. I read about him in the local newspaper. Besides, look at the way she's clinging to him now. It looks to me as if there's something sleazy going on between them two."

Grace blinked. "Whatcha mean, sleazy?"

"You know." Olivia nudged her with an elbow and winked. "Him and her sleazy."

"But he's married!" Grace stared at the couple in disbelief. "And he's years older than her."

Olivia smiled. "I know."

Uncomfortable now, Grace tugged at her friend's sleeve. "Come on. I thought you wanted to join the protest." She tilted her head to one side. "I think I can hear them now."

"Oh, cripes. Come on." Olivia grabbed Grace's hand and charged around the corner. All Grace could do was follow, and hope to the heavens that they could stay out of trouble.

After having been met with nothing but skepticism from the other instructresses, Meredith decided to keep to herself her experience in the flower gardens. Obviously Kathleen was worried that her precious flowers would not be taken care of properly now that she had departed.

Meredith had read somewhere that spirits were sometimes unable to pass on because of some unfinished business, and that once those concerns had been taken care of, the spirit was then free to cross over into the hereafter.

Not that she had attached any significance to that notion. At least, not until now. If she were honest with herself, she'd admit that she was not entirely convinced that what she had seen was anything other than a trick of her mind, brought about by her grief at losing such a valued friend and associate.

Nevertheless, she fully intended to keep her promise to Kathleen. That afternoon she searched the grounds until she found Tom in the far corner of the playing field, measuring the tennis nets in order to ensure they were the correct height for the finals tournament.

"I happened to notice," she began, as he touched his forehead with his fingers, "that the flower beds are in need of a good weeding. I'm quite sure it's an oversight on your part, but Miss Duncan was so particular about her flower beds. I know you would want to keep them in excellent shape as a tribute to her memory."

Tom took off his hat and scratched the back of his head. "I sent Davie to weed them," he muttered. "Don't know why he didn't do it."

Remembering the young lad's stricken face, Meredith said quietly, "He's most likely suffering from shock over Miss Duncan's death. Perhaps you could have a word with him? Tell him that he would be doing Miss Duncan a great service by keeping her flower beds neat, and free from weeds."

Tom shook his head. "Doubt that would do any good, m'm. I don't think he's feeling too kindly toward Miss Duncan at the moment. She scolded the lad for picking flowers last week. He'd picked them to give to her. It were supposed to be a surprise. After she told him off, he went off by hisself and he ain't been the same since."

Meredith stared at him. "I'm sorry to hear that. I'm quite sure Miss Duncan would have understood if she'd known. We all know the boy is bashful, and she wouldn't have wanted to hurt his feelings that way."

Again Tom shrugged. "There's no telling with youngsters these days. I'll get on him to weed the gardens. He'll do it fast enough if I threaten to sack him."

"Oh, I wouldn't want you to do that." Meredith raised her head as the sound of the school bell echoed across the field. "Please, just tell him I would like him to weed the beds. I'll have a word with him myself next time I see him."

"Very well." Tom pulled his hat on his head again, and Meredith hurried away. Poor Davie. Kathleen had a sharp tongue at times. Meredith decided she would have to make sure to be gentle with him when she saw him again.

Arriving back at the school, she found Felicity waiting for her in the hallway.

"We'll have to find a replacement for Kathleen as soon as possible," she announced, as soon as Meredith was within earshot. "Essie is doing her best but honestly, what does she know about home management? She's never had to think for herself in her entire life, much less run a household."

"Well, she won't have to take Kathleen's class after today." Meredith hunted in her pocket for the key to her office. "We have a replacement starting tomorrow."

Felicity stared at her in surprise. "How did you manage that so quickly?"

"I didn't. Mr. Hamilton hired the new instructress. He seems to think she's qualified and experienced." She pretended to examine the key in her hand in an attempt to avoid Felicity's shrewd gaze.

"Ah, the charming Mr. Hamilton." Felicity snorted. "I suppose you had no objection to him taking matters into his own hands without consulting us?"

Meredith winced. "I'm aware that it was a little presumptuous, but he is the owner of Bellehaven and so I suppose he should have the last word."

"The last word, perhaps, but certainly not the first and only word. Obviously he regards all of us as lowly teachers who can't be trusted to judge the qualifications of an associate. Really!"

"I'm quite sure he had no intention of insulting our intelligence—"

"Oh, bosh, Meredith." Felicity jammed her hands into the pockets of her skirt. "In every other matter you have a strong mind of your own, yet all that man has to do is raise his little finger and you crumble. If I didn't know better, I'd wager you have a fancy for that arrogant creature."

Meredith's laugh strangled in her throat. "Don't be absurd, Felicity. As I said, Stuart Hamilton owns this school and has a perfect right to dictate the way this establishment is run, as well as who shall work here. As headmistress I'm obligated to bow to his wishes. In any case, I trust his judgment. I'm quite certain Miss Montrose will be an admirable addition to our faculty."

"Well, I hope you're right." Felicity turned away so sharply her skirt swished about her ankles. "These girls only have to sniff weakness in a tutor and they'll take full advantage. I hope your precious Mr. Hamilton and his protégée are fully aware of the effort it takes to keep them under control."

She stalked off, leaving Meredith ruefully shaking her head. She was used to Felicity's abrasiveness and paid no attention to it, but she had to agree with her sentiments. Stuart Hamilton had no idea the effort it took to control the students. She could only share Felicity's hope that Miss Montrose was up to the task.

Chapter 6

Outside the town hall a swarm of women jostled each other to get a footing on the wide stone steps. Their voices rose in a clamor of chanting slogans and shouts of outrage, unsettling more than one horse as they trotted past the unruly group.

Grace stayed close to Olivia's side, terrified they'd be separated by the angry women. Why she'd ever agreed to come on this ridiculous escapade she couldn't imagine. They were going to end up in prison. She just knew it.

She could hear Olivia chanting something, but couldn't make out the words. Not that she wanted to understand them. All she wanted was to get out of there and go back where they belonged. These women scared her, with their wild eyes and harsh voices.

Someone thrust a post in her hands. "Here," the woman said, her cheeks a fiery red, "take this and get up to the door. You're younger than me. My old legs won't carry me past that mob."

Grace looked up at the placard in her hands. It said "Votes for Women" in large letters and underneath that in smaller letters it said, "Down with Parliament!"

Treason. That's what it was. Terrified, Grace tried to give the placard back to the woman but she'd disappeared in the crowd. Twisting her head, Grace did her best to catch Olivia's eye, but she was staring up the steps at the three women near the door. They stood with arms linked and seemed to be urging the rest of the women to shout louder.

If it got any louder, Grace thought, she'd go completely deaf. She tried to edge closer to Olivia, but a couple of hefty women blocked her way, and the heavy placard slowed her down. She tried yelling at Olivia, but her voice got lost in the roar from the crowd.

A commotion off to her right caught her attention. She heard screams, men shouting, women swearing in a most unladylike way. She tried to see what was going on, and not for the first time cursed her lack of height. She couldn't see Olivia now, as the women pushed closer together, all trying to see where the uproar was coming from.

Then suddenly, the women parted right in front of Grace. She was about to step into the space when someone else loomed up in front of her. With a frantically beating heart, Grace looked up into the stern face of a constable. In his raised hand he held a thick black baton.

She uttered a squeal of fright and without thinking, thrust the cumbersome placard right into the bobby's chest. With a shout he staggered backward, tripped over a woman behind him and crashed to the ground.

Grace took one horrified look at his furious face, then turned and plunged into the crowd. By some miracle she spied Olivia on the lower step and grabbed her by the hand.

At first Olivia resisted her tugging, until Grace gasped, "Quick! I knocked a bobby over. He's coming after me!"

Olivia's eyes widened. "What on earth did you go and do that for?"

"I didn't mean to—" Grace froze as a man's deep voice shouted out behind her.

Olivia leapt from the step and together they fought their way through the struggling women until they reached the corner of the street. After one quick look back at the struggle going on behind them, they lifted their skirts and ran.

Meredith paused in front of a fidgety student and frowned at the lumpy pile of clay in front of her. Normally Amelia Webster was a model student—talented as well as intelligent—but this afternoon she appeared to have lost all control of her nimble fingers.

"I see you have hardly begun your sculpture." Meredith prodded the offending lump with her finger. "Is something wrong? Are you not well?"

Amelia kept her head down when she answered. "I'm quite well, Mrs. Llewellyn, thank you."

Now that she really looked at the girl, Meredith noticed her cheeks were quite flushed. Concerned that she might be taken ill, she laid her palm on the girl's forehead.

Amelia jerked back as if she'd been stung.

Meredith looked at her in surprise. "There's no need for alarm. I was merely testing your forehead to see if you had a raised temperature."

Amelia promptly burst into tears.

The girl seated next to her leaned over and patted her arm. "She's upset over what happened to Miss Duncan," she said, with just a tinge of reproach in her voice. "We all are."

Of course. How insensitive she had been. Meredith felt a twinge of guilt. She had been so engrossed in her own problems she had failed to consider that Kathleen's pupils might not have recovered from the shock of their teacher's death.

She walked to the front of the class and cleared her throat. "I share your grief over losing our beloved instructress. Miss Duncan was very fond of you all, and I know you all cared just as much about her."

"Not really," one of the girls muttered. "Not when she shouted at us, we didn't." She glanced over at Amelia. "I don't know why you're crying over her, Amy. Remember how she screeched at you when you brought weeds instead of flowers to class? You were upset all day long."

Some of the girls tittered behind their hands. Amelia sobbed louder, and dabbed at her nose with a white, lacy handkerchief.

"Made her look really stupid," the girl told her companion seated next to her.

The companion snickered, then cut it off when Meredith glared at her. "I'm sure everyone has borne the brunt of Miss Duncan's tongue lashings at one time or another. That doesn't make our grief for her passing any less painful. I'm sure we all miss her dreadfully."

Two or three heads nodded solemnly in agreement.

Meredith decided this was a good time to impart the good news. "I'm happy to tell you that a replacement has been found, and that Miss Sylvia Montrose will arrive at Bellehaven tomorrow morning. She will be taking over Miss Duncan's classes in home management. I'm sure you will all make her feel welcome, and I trust you will do your best to ease her transition into Bellehaven."

Whispers hissed about the room until Meredith held up

her hand. "There is just one more thing. We would very much like to know more of the details of how Miss Duncan died. If anyone remembers seeing her that evening or has any knowledge that might be helpful, I'd appreciate it if you would come to tell me. We would like to know as much as possible about her last moments."

Aware of the curious glances sent her way, Meredith hurried to add, "For her family, of course. I'm sure they'll want to know exactly what happened."

"Reggie said someone hit Miss Duncan on the head with a branch," a voice declared from the back of the room.

Shocked gasps greeted this startling statement, while Meredith glared at the girl who'd delivered it. "It is unwise to pay attention to gossip," she said, inwardly cursing Reggie's loose tongue. "One rarely gets the truth from such an unreliable source."

"Then it's a lie?"

Meredith hesitated. "Since Miss Duncan was apparently alone, we have no way of knowing what happened. Which is why I would like to talk to anyone who might have seen her walking the grounds that evening."

"Maybe she was meeting with a suitor," someone said, earning snickers from several of her closest companions.

"I think that's extremely unlikely," Meredith said sharply. Though she had to confess, the idea had merit. Perhaps Kathleen had planned to meet someone that evening. Someone who had taken advantage of the darkness to strike her down.

Another girl timidly held up her hand. "Do you think someone from the school killed Miss Duncan?"

The bell rang at that moment, saving Meredith from answering. Uneasily she watched the girls file out in sobering silence. *Someone from the school?* Good Lord, she prayed that wasn't so. It was unfortunate that the seeds of doubt had now been sewn among the pupils.

Then again, it would have been only a matter of time before word got out. If knowing the truth helped find out who had attacked Kathleen, however, perhaps it wasn't entirely a bad thing.

The dining hall was exceptionally quiet that evening throughout supper. The pupils spoke to each other in low voices, without the laughter that normally punctuated their conversation. It was as if a cloud of doom had settled over the students of Bellehaven, and Meredith was very much afraid that it would remain there until the mystery of Kathleen's death had been uncovered.

Although she waited in her office for quite some time after supper, no one appeared to report having seen Kathleen the evening she died. Frustrated by her lack of progress, Meredith could do nothing but retire to her room for an early night. The new day would bring the new teacher, and yet another set of problems.

After rising early the following morning, she took her usual stroll in the gardens before breakfast. The walk helped clear her head and prepare her for the long day.

Telling herself that she needed to make sure the weeding had been done, she tingled with expectation as she approached the flower beds. Tom was nowhere to be seen, for which she felt relieved. It seemed that Kathleen only visited her when she was quite alone.

Having had no success so far in her quest to find out the truth, she hoped to see Kathleen's apparition again. Much as the idea unnerved her, she felt compelled to communicate with Kathleen's ghost.

For one thing, she needed to know that she was still of sound mind, and that her visions were real and not caused by some malfunction of her brain.

Then again, perhaps this time she could actually converse with Kathleen's ghost, though she had no idea how one went about such things.

Since she had no previous experience with the spiritual world, she was rather at a loss about how to proceed. Nothing had prepared her for such an implausible situation.

To make matters worse, she was completely alone in this bizarre quest. She could go to no one for help, since nobody believed she could see a ghost. She still found it impossible to believe herself.

Moreover, if word should get back to the school board, or worse, Stuart Hamilton, that she was having hallucinations, she could very well lose her position as headmistress.

It was all extremely disturbing.

Braced for the appearance of Kathleen's cloud, it was almost an anticlimax when the patch of mist finally formed at the edge of the flower beds.

Meredith felt the usual jolt of dread at the first sight of it, but this time she recovered far more quickly. By the time she could make out Kathleen's face, she felt almost calm.

"Give me a sign," she hissed at her friend, as the ghostly figure faded in and out like a shadow caught between sunlight and cloud. "What are you trying to tell me?"

The ghost seemed to understand, as one arm raised and a long finger pointed once more at the flowers.

Meredith stared at the blossoms in frustration. The beds had been weeded after all, so it was not the weeds that concerned Kathleen.

Another idea raised her head. "Are you concerned about your classes? Worried about your pupils? There's no need.

We have a new teacher arriving today. Stuart Hamilton se-
lected her himself. I'm sure she'll—"

The ghost appeared to be agitated. The arm fluttered,
then before Meredith could draw another breath, the mist
faded away and disappeared.

Disappointed, she turned away, then paused as a faint
sound, carried by the breeze, drifted from the silent trees.
The sound of someone crying.

She hurried toward the pitiful sobbing, but as she drew
near a figure moved in the shadows. He slipped away to
vanish among the trees, but not quickly enough to hide his
face. It was Davie Gray.

"Miss Fingle wants to see you two in her office this
morning." Mrs. Wilkins laid a stern eye on Olivia. "I told
you not to go to Witchaton yesterday. Now you're both in
a lot of trouble."

Olivia shrugged, while Grace's face filled with alarm.
Neither girl answered, which worried Mrs. Wilkins more
than anything they might have said.

She stared hard into Grace's face, knowing the girl was
far more likely to tell her what she wanted to know. "So
what happened yesterday, anyway?"

Grace glanced at Olivia, whose expression clearly
warned her to keep her mouth shut. "Nothing happened,
Mrs. Wilkins," she said weakly.

The cook pinched her lips together. "Something must
have happened. I didn't hear you come in last night, so you
must have got back really late. What were you doing all
day?"

"Protesting," Olivia said, with a toss of her head. "That's
why we went, wasn't it. To protest."

Mrs. Wilkins studied Grace's face and saw guilt written all over it. "I want to know what happened," she said quietly, "and you're not going anywhere until you tell me."

Grace looked frightened, and tears started spilling down her cheeks. "We nearly got arrested, that's what."

Olivia turned on her with an explosive sound of fury. "I told you not to say anything!"

Mrs. Wilkins folded her arms and summoned her strictest voice. "I think you'd better tell me everything that happened, because sooner or later I'm going to find out."

"Grace punched a constable in the belly and knocked him down," Olivia bellowed. "There! Is that what you wanted to know?"

Grace started whimpering.

Shocked, Mrs. Wilkins stared at her. "Why on earth did you do that?"

"I didn't mean to," Grace wailed. "I sort of bumped into him with the sign I was carrying and he sort of tripped and fell down."

"Oh, good Lord." Mrs. Wilkins felt for the chair behind her and sat down hard.

"He didn't catch us." Olivia sounded sullen now. "We ran away and he chased us—"

"So did lots of people," Grace added, wiping her wet nose on her sleeve. "We had to run really, really hard to get away."

"And then we had to hide in a coal shed." Olivia fished a handkerchief out of her sleeve and shoved it at Grace. "Until it got dark enough to come out again."

Mrs. Wilkins winced when Grace trumpeted into the square of white cotton. "Mercy me. So how did you get home?"

"We walked and walked," Grace said, handing the

handkerchief back to Olivia. "I thought I was going to drop, I did."

"But then we heard a cart coming up behind us." Olivia tucked the handkerchief back in her sleeve. "It was one of the farmers and he offered us a ride. So we hopped aboard."

"Our clothes are all dirty." Grace held up her hands. "I scrubbed and scrubbed but I still have coal dust under my fingernails."

"We'd better get that out before you see Miss Fingle." Mrs. Wilkins got up and pulled the girl over to the sink. "And if I were you, I'd keep quiet about that constable."

She could hear the relief in Olivia's voice when she asked, "So you're not going to tell her?"

"You're in enough trouble already." Mrs. Wilkins held Grace's fingers under the tap and let the cold water run while she scrubbed. "Miss Fingle will probably take away your afternoons off for a month."

Olivia muttered something she didn't catch. "Well, we're not the only ones in trouble," she added. "We saw one of the pupils from here having a big row with Victor Silkwood right in the middle of the street. If you ask me, he's probably going to report her to Mrs. Llewellyn. I wouldn't want to be in that girl's shoes when the headmistress finds out."

Mrs. Wilkins frowned. "Which pupil was that, then?"

"Don't know her name."

Grace uttered a squeak of protest as Mrs. Wilkins dug under her nails with a toothpick.

The cook let her go, and turned off the tap. "There, that's the best I can do. Now go and face the music with Miss Fingle, then you both come right back here. You've got a lot to catch up on."

She watched the girls trudge out the door, but her mind was on the girl Olivia had mentioned. Why in heaven's name would a Bellehaven girl be crossing swords with one of the richest men in the county? She couldn't be his daughter, since everyone knew the Silkwoods had no daughters. Moreover, Mrs. Wilkins knew every pupil in the school, and as far as she knew, none of them were related to the prominent family.

A notable connection such as that would certainly be blazoned all over the school, and while Mrs. Wilkins would be the last person to admit she was a gossip, she was rather proud of her ability to know everyone and everything that went on under the illustrious roofs of Bellehaven.

Deciding that perhaps she should have a word with Mrs. Llewellyn about the incident, she turned her attention to that day's main meal.

Chapter 7

Sylvia Montrose arrived in the middle of the morning, accompanied by a startling amount of baggage. Meredith felt quite sorry for poor Reggie, who struggled
valiantly to haul a large trunk and several valises up the
stairs to the new teacher's chamber.

Miss Montrose appeared younger and decidedly more
comely than Meredith had envisioned—a fact that rather
irritated her, though she couldn't imagine why.

The new instructress spoke in a soft voice that was at
times difficult to hear, with a slight lisp that was bound to
invite trouble from some of the more unruly students.

She had a way of twitching her eyes about, as if inspect-
ing her surroundings. Judging from her expression, Bellehaven fell rather short of her expectations.

Confused to find herself so defensive, Meredith made
an extra effort to be accommodating. She waited for an
hour in order to allow Miss Montrose to settle in, before
politely tapping on her door.

It opened immediately, and she was relieved to note that Miss Montrose seemed a little less disparaging as she greeted her.

"I thought you might like to meet some of your students," Meredith said, after she had conducted a short tour of the school. "I asked Miss Cross to take your class this morning, and I'm quite sure she'll be delighted to see you."

"Likewise," Sylvia murmured in her soft voice. "I'm anxious to begin teaching."

"Mr. Hamilton tells me you are quite experienced," Meredith said, as she led the other woman down the long corridor. "He mentioned that you were very well recommended."

Personally, she thought Sylvia Montrose looked too young to be either. Her appearance—the fresh face and smooth skin, the slim figure and the lightness of her step—suggested the woman wasn't much older than Essie. The fact that Sylvia was not yet married added weight to that assumption.

"I have tutored quite a few children in many subjects," Sylvia murmured.

Meredith wondered what that had to do with managing a household, but held her tongue. She had to assume that Stuart Hamilton knew what he was doing. "You may find the pupils at Bellehaven quite different from the charges to whom you are accustomed." She paused in front of a classroom door. "I'm afraid young ladies can be spirited and somewhat rebellious at times."

As if to confirm her sentiments, raised voices could be heard from the other side of the door. Felicity's strident tones rose above the rest, as if attempting to be heard above the clamor.

Reluctant to present her friend in an unfavorable light, Meredith dropped her hand from the doorknob. "Perhaps this isn't a good time. It might be as well to wait until after the midday meal."

Sylvia raised her chin, and with surprising firmness declared, "I should very much like to go in there now." Without waiting for Meredith's consent, she grasped the doorknob and turned it.

The door swung open to a deafening commotion. Meredith smothered a gasp when she saw Felicity marching back and forth in front of the class, punching the air with her fist while she chanted, "Women are power! Down with men! Women are power! Down with men!"

Her students roared in approval, clapping and leaping about in a frenzy of excitement. Some of the girls stood on chairs, and one young woman actually bounced up and down on top of her desk in a manner more befitting a common harlot than a future debutante.

The noise was so great and the exhilaration so fierce that no one appeared to notice Meredith and her companion in the doorway.

For several seconds they stood there, stunned into silence. It was Sylvia who recovered first. She bounded forward, right in front of Felicity's path and stood there, hands on hips, green eyes blazing.

Meredith had to admit, with her reddish blond hair catching the sunlight that streamed through the window, the woman presented quite a magnificent spectacle.

Certainly enough to stop Felicity's rampage. Cutting off her chant, she halted in front of the irate Miss Montrose demanding, "Who the blazes are you?"

Instead of answering her, Sylvia turned to the girls, some of whom still hadn't noticed the newcomers to the room and were chanting over and over, "Down with men! Down with the government!"

All traces of a lisp vanished as Sylvia screeched, "Stop this nonsense at once!"

For the first time Felicity noticed Meredith and had the grace to look sheepish. Felicity held up her hands and roared at the top of her voice, "All right, you hooligans! Silence! Right *now*!"

Gradually the voices died down, until only the shuffling of feet could be heard.

Meredith waited until the fidgeting ceased, then said quietly, "This is Miss Montrose, your new instructress for home management. I trust you will pay her attention and make her feel welcome."

She fixed a stern gaze on each of the now silent girls facing her. "I fully expect everyone to treat Miss Montrose with the respect and consideration afforded all the teachers here at Bellehaven."

She stepped back and signaled to Sylvia to address the class. Felicity looked as if she would speak, but Meredith shook her head at her. To her relief, Felicity snapped her mouth shut and also drew back.

The pupils stared at Sylvia, apparently assessing their new teacher. She seemed to have calmed her temper, though a bright spot of pink stained each of her cheeks. Her long lashes fluttered for a moment or two while she appeared to collect herself, then she started speaking, her voice once more soft and mellow.

"I am delighted to be accepted here at Bellehaven. I relish the opportunity to instruct young ladies in the proper way to manage a household, and I have many exciting ideas and projects that I hope you will all find entertaining as well as educational."

She then launched into a summary of her curriculum and her expectations of the class. "By the time you finish these courses," she added, "you will be able to advise your domestic staff so that your home runs smoothly and efficiently. You will excel in catering extravagant parties that your guests will talk about for years to come. You will learn how to be the perfect companion to your future husband, interpret his wishes, and obey his commands, thus providing a sanctuary worthy of his excellence."

"Poppycock!" Felicity said loudly.

Meredith winced as Sylvia turned to her, both cheeks burning once more. "I beg your pardon?"

"I said poppycock!" Brushing aside Meredith's restraining hand, Felicity strode to Sylvia's side. "It is one thing to instruct these young women how to supervise staff and make important decisions concerning the running of their households, but I will not stand by while you urge them to submit to slavery."

Sylvia's eyes opened wide. "Slavery? Whatever do you mean?"

"I mean all this unmitigated nonsense you're spouting about bowing and scraping in front of their husbands. Obey his commands, indeed. Good Lord, woman, you will put the women's movement back a hundred years!"

A militant expression crossed Sylvia's face. "So that's it. You are one of those abominable suffragettes. I'm surprised and disappointed to find someone with your questionable beliefs allowed anywhere close to these impressionable young girls, much less to actually educate them. I had expected more from this institution."

Watching Felicity's spine stiffen, Meredith decided it was time to intervene before the pupils witnessed an unseemly confrontation. They were already showing signs of enjoying the dispute a little too much.

"Now look here—" Felicity began, but Meredith forestalled her.

"Miss Montrose," she said, clamping down hard on Felicity's arm as a warning. "Here at Bellehaven we are open to all points of view, though we are careful not to advocate any one of them. The more the students are exposed to this changing world, the more aware they will be of their choices. We encourage them to analyze and consider all possibilities in the belief that they will then be capable of making wise decisions when faced with life's complications."

Sylvia's eyes were like twin icebergs glowing in a winter sea. "May I suggest that such a policy could encourage the girls to open rebellion against their teachers?"

Felicity snorted, but mercifully held her tongue.

"A good teacher will know how to balance her presentations." Meredith tempered her words with a smile. "While we certainly do not sanction rebellion, we do encourage the students to value their own opinions and beliefs. That policy has always worked well for us, and I trust it will continue to do so."

For several seconds the new teacher continued to stare into Meredith's eyes, while it seemed everyone in the room held their breath. Then Sylvia spoke.

"Very well, I will keep your observations in mind. I shall, however, continue to hold to my own beliefs, and maintain my right to present them. Within the boundaries of your policies, of course."

Meredith nodded. "That seems satisfactory. I appreciate your understanding. Thank you." Keeping her grip on

Felicity's arm, she pulled her toward the door. "Class, you will conduct yourselves in the manner befitting your station." With that she made as dignified an exit as possible, considering she had Felicity in tow.

Once outside, she faced her friend. "What in heaven's name were you thinking?"

Felicity shrugged. "Someone mentioned the suffragette movement and things escalated from there." She shook her head. "That frumpish new teacher is going to undo all the good work I've done with those girls." She waved a hand at the classroom door. "Look at her. She's probably insisting right now that they disregard everything I've ever taught them."

Meredith studied Sylvia through the glass window. "As a matter of fact, she's instructing them on the latest designs in tableware."

Felicity grunted. "Your ability to read lips so efficiently never fails to astonish me. How did you come by such a dubious trait, anyway?"

"I learned the habit as a child, as I've already told you. It came in very useful when I wanted to know what the grown-ups were saying when they thought I was out of earshot." Meredith shook her head. "Don't change the subject. You came close to instigating a riot in there. In front of our new instructress, as well. I just know she'll go to Stuart Hamilton with this. He'll be most displeased."

Felicity sniffed. "Is that what you're concerned about? That Hamilton will think poorly of us? Well, let him! He might own this school, but he has no say in the way we conduct our classes."

"He does have a say in who remains here as an instructress, however." Meredith frowned at her. "I should hate to give him cause to question the integrity of any one of us."

Felicity smiled. "You worry far too much, Meredith. Like this business over Kathleen's death. I know how much you miss her, but she's gone, and there's nothing you can do to help her now. Once the funeral is over tomorrow and she is finally buried, you will feel better, I promise you."

Meredith seriously doubted that. In fact, she felt a sense of urgency, as if she had to find out who was responsible for Kathleen's death before her friend's coffin was lowered into the ground.

Maybe that's what Kathleen wanted, too. She should have realized that earlier. Could it be that Kathleen was trying to tell her who had killed her? The idea was so unsettling, she gasped out loud.

Felicity paused, and looked back at her. "What is it? Tummy ache? Always happens to me when I get upset. I have some milk of magnesia in my room. That usually helps calm the collywobbles."

For a moment Meredith was tempted to share her revelation, then thought better of it. Convincing her friend that Kathleen's ghost existed was as feasible as flying to the moon. "Just a momentary twinge in my stomach," she assured her. "It's gone now."

"You need to eat." Felicity took hold of her arm. "Come, let us see what Mrs. Wilkins is cooking up for us. It's almost mealtime anyway."

Meredith allowed herself to be pulled toward the kitchen, though her appetite seemed to have deserted her. She needed time to think. Somewhere in her brief encounters with Kathleen's ghost, she felt certain there lay a clue that would guide her to whoever had attacked her friend and left her to die all alone. Now she had to determine what that clue was, and where it would lead.

Mrs. Wilkins greeted them both when they entered the

warm, fragrant kitchen. After offering them a hot cup of a tea and a buttered scone, she turned to Meredith. "I've been meaning to have a word with you, Mrs. Llewellyn. It has to do with my maids."

"Oh, dear." Seated at the table, Meredith sipped a mouthful of tea and replaced the cup in its saucer. "What trouble are they in now?"

Mrs. Wilkins shook her head in mock despair. "Playing truant, that's what. Miss Fingle punished them by taking away their days off this week and next, but that's not what I wanted to tell you." She glanced at Felicity, as if wary of continuing in front of her.

"Fire ahead." Felicity waved her half-eaten scone at her. "I won't interfere."

Seemingly reassured by Meredith's nod of agreement, Mrs. Wilkins dug in the pocket of her apron and pulled out a handkerchief. After blowing her nose, she tucked it back out of sight. "Well, it's like this. Olivia says they saw one of our pupils having a nasty argument with Mr. Silkwood out on the street. Going at it hammer and tongs, they was, according to Olivia."

Meredith stared at her. "Victor Silkwood? Who was the girl?"

"Olivia didn't know her name. Just that she recognized her as coming from Bellehaven. I wouldn't have thought twice about it, except I wouldn't want there to be any trouble with Mr. Silkwood and the school, seeing as how he's on the council, and all."

"Quite," Meredith murmured. Victor Silkwood was a major influence, both on the school board and in the county council office. If he complained about the school or its residents, that would bring Stuart Hamilton's wrath down on her head. It was the last thing she needed right now. "I'll have a word with Olivia when she's finished with her chores. She may be able to describe the girl."

"Well, I wouldn't hold out too much hope of that." Mrs. Wilkins turned back to the table and started kneading a mound of pastry on the floured board. "Empty-headed the two of them. I don't know which one's worse. Olivia, the ring leader, or Grace, the faithful follower."

Meredith finished her tea and put down the cup. "Well, it won't hurt to try."

Felicity got up and had reached the door when Mrs. Wilkins answered, "Nearly got arrested, they did. Joined in that suffragette protest in Witcheston. Grace knocked down a bobby and they had to run for their lives."

Felicity's face lit up. "Well, there's more gumption to those girls than I'd thought."

"Well, lucky for them no one caught them. Spent most of the day stuck in a coal cellar and had to walk half the way home, they did."

Meredith frowned. "I sincerely hope the experience taught them a lesson."

"I doubt it. Couple of daredevils, them two are. Don't know what they'll be up to next, that I don't."

"I'm sure you'll be able to manage them." Meredith rose from her chair. "Thank you, Mrs. Wilkins. The scones were delicious, as always."

She followed Felicity, who sailed out the door and didn't stop smiling until after they parted company at the top of the stairs.

The tiny church was filled to capacity the following afternoon. Meredith sat between Felicity and Essie as usual, and couldn't seem to tear her gaze away from Kathleen's empty spot in the front pew. It was difficult to imagine the body of her dear friend lying lifeless inside the flower-draped coffin at the altar.

She kept hoping the ghost would appear, though she had no idea how she would communicate with her in full view of the congregation. It seemed the whole town had attended the service to commemorate Kathleen's passing.

The overcast sky cast a gloom over the graveyard as the coffin was lowered into its final resting place. It seemed to Meredith as if even the sun mourned the death of the beloved woman.

The pupils, all fifty of them, stood with bowed heads in respectful silence. Kathleen would have been most gratified to see that.

Mrs. Wilkins had set up a lavish array of refreshments in the assembly hall, and people milled about, mingling with the pupils and talking in hushed voices.

Meredith was in no mood to socialize and after a decent interval, excused herself and left to retire to her room. On the way there she caught up with Sylvia Montrose, who also appeared to be retiring.

"So sad," Sylvia said, when Meredith greeted her. "I didn't know the lady, but I can see how much she was admired and respected."

"Kathleen Duncan was loved by a good many people." Meredith fell in step beside Sylvia as they made their way down the long corridor to the stairs. "She was dedicated to her work at Bellehaven. She will be missed."

"It will be difficult to follow in her footsteps."

Sylvia sounded subdued, and Meredith felt quite sorry for her. "I'm sure you will be more than capable. After all, you are at liberty to set your own patterns, and instill your own methods. The only thing I ask is that you teach flower arranging in your class. Kathleen loved her flowers so. In fact, she could get quite—" She broke off as a thought suddenly occurred to her.

Sylvia looked at her with curious eyes. "Quite what?"

"Oh." Meredith collected herself. "I was going to say that Kathleen could get quite irritated with anyone who mistreated her beloved blossoms." She smiled at Sylvia. "If you will excuse me, I've just remembered something that needs my immediate attention."

She hurried off, aware that Sylvia Montrose stared after her in confusion. Not that it bothered her for long. Talking about Kathleen's love of flowers had jogged her memory. She remembered a comment made by one of Kathleen's charges.

The teacher had been incensed when one of her pupils had mistaken weeds for flowers. So much so that in church on Sunday morning Meredith had remembered her friend complaining about it the night before—the same night she had been murdered.

Kathleen had also mentioned at the time that she intended to give Amelia Webster a favorite book of hers on flowers in the hopes the girl would learn to identify them more clearly.

If she had done so, it was possible that Amelia was the last person to see Kathleen alive. She must have a word with her just as soon as possible.

Chapter 8

Meredith seized the opportunity to talk to Amelia when she caught sight of the girl leaving the assembly hall with a group of friends. To spare the young woman any awkward moments, she followed at a discreet distance until Amelia entered her room, then tapped on the door.

Amelia answered at once, her smile vanishing when she saw her visitor. She held onto the door as if determined not to let it go.

"I'd like a word with you, Amelia." Meredith gave her an encouraging smile. "May I come in?"

"Yes, of course, miss." She opened the door and stepped back.

Meredith stepped into the room, relieved to see they were alone. She wasted no time in coming to the point. "As you know, I'm trying to find out if anyone saw Miss Duncan leave the building on Saturday night. She mentioned earlier that evening that she intended to give you a book about flowers."

Amelia nodded vigorously. "Yes, miss, she did. A lovely book." She looked concerned. "Should I give it back?"

"Oh, no, I'm sure Miss Duncan would have wanted you to keep it." Meredith glanced around the room, noting the neatly made bed and uncluttered dresser. A hat sat in front of the mirror, its wide brim adorned with blue ribbons and tiny butterflies nestled among enormous white lace daisies.

Having been momentarily distracted, Meredith brought her gaze back to Amelia, who stood waiting in obvious anticipation for her next words.

"Pardon me," Meredith said hurriedly. "I came to ask if Miss Duncan happened to mention where she was going when she left you."

"I'm sorry, but I don't remember her saying anything of the sort."

"And you didn't see her again after she left your room?"

"No, I didn't." Amelia met her gaze steadily. "Loretta, my room partner, was here when Miss Duncan left. We spent the whole evening in here together while I studied the flower book. She might remember if Miss Duncan mentioned where she was going."

Meredith frowned. "Loretta Davenport?"

"Yes, miss."

"Well, thank you, Amelia." She peered at the girl. "I hope you're feeling a little better about Miss Duncan's death?"

Amelia dropped her gaze to the floor. "Yes, miss. Thank you."

Meredith studied her for a moment longer, then turned to leave.

"Oh, Mrs. Llewellyn?"

Meredith twisted her head to look at her. "Yes?"

"I just remembered something." Amelia twisted a strand of her blond hair around her finger. "I heard someone crying in the corridor outside my room that evening. I opened the door to see who it was, and I saw Penelope Fisher running down the hallway."

Meredith pictured the tomboyish girl with flying pigtails. One of her problem students. She seemed determined to hang on to her adolescence and resented all attempts to change her into a young lady. Somehow, Meredith had a great deal of trouble picturing her crying. Penelope was far too invincible to easily succumb to tears.

"Penelope Fisher? Are you quite sure?"

"Yes, miss. I called out after her but she didn't hear me. I suppose she was too upset. I did wonder at the time what troubled her so."

"Well, thank you, Amelia." Meredith left the room, her mind juggling thoughts. Obviously something had happened to deeply disturb Penelope. She would have to question the girl. As for Amelia, her answers seemed straightforward enough, but Meredith couldn't escape the feeling that the girl was trying to hide something from her.

She hurried back along the corridor, intent on reaching her room. This detective business was a lot harder than she'd imagined. The more questions she asked, the more confusing everything became. It just didn't seem feasible that no one saw Kathleen that evening.

There was always the possibility that Penelope had witnessed the murder and was too afraid to tell anyone. If that were so, Meredith reflected, she'd have to be very careful how she questioned her.

Thinking of Penelope weeping reminded her of Davie, who had also cried. Might he have seen something and was keeping quiet about it?

Deep in thought, she failed to see Stuart Hamilton until she'd almost bumped into him. He stood at the base of the staircase, one foot planted on the first of the steps as if he were about to climb them.

"There you are, Mrs. Llewellyn." His deep voice echoed down the corridor behind her, and a shiver touched her spine. "I was just on my way to talk to you."

She'd seen him moving among the mourners in the ballroom, but had managed to avoid meeting up with him. Now, it seemed, she had no choice. "Mr. Hamilton. I trust you are well?"

He ignored her question. "I wanted a word with you. Miss Montrose has some concerns about Miss Cross. Apparently she tends to incite the pupils, and this morning they disrupted the class."

Meredith mentally cursed Sylvia's tattling. "An unfortunate misunderstanding, that's all." She made herself meet Hamilton's piercing gaze. "I can assure you, Mr Hamilton, it won't happen again."

In spite of her best efforts to remain indifferent, she found herself fascinated by the way he pursed his lips before answering her. "I understand Miss Cross is a staunch supporter of the women's movement. I trust her views have no bearing on the policies and procedures of Bellehaven?"

Meredith hastily adjusted her gaze. "None at all, I can assure you. We are here to ensure our pupils meet their future obligations with proficiency, integrity, and wisdom. That is the mission of Bellehaven, and we strive to uphold it. Nothing more."

"So, you do not encourage these young ladies to rebel against the very hand that feeds them? You do not condone the view that women should destroy property and languish in prisons in their efforts to gain the right to vote?"

Meredith noticed one dark eyebrow twitch. Could the dratted man possibly be poking fun at her? "What I personally

believe is my own business," she said, her voice clipped. "It
has nothing to do with the way our business at Bellehaven is
conducted."

"Very glad to hear it." Hamilton bowed his head, though
not before Meredith had caught the gleam of amusement
in his eyes. "I bid you an exceptional good night, Mrs.
Lewellyn."

"Likewise, Mr. Hamilton."

She allowed him to pass, then stomped up the stairs. Infuriating man! Why was it she felt at such a disadvantage
whenever faced with his impudence?

Despite her irritation, she managed to accomplish much
of the work that awaited her in her room. Now that Kathleen was no longer there to help her, the paperwork seemed
to be piling up at an alarming rate.

After entering the marks in the ledger, she studied the
results of the tests she had set her pupils the day before. It
seemed that her charges had paid attention to her lectures
on van Gogh and Gauguin.

The favorable outcome of her endeavors mellowed her
mood, and she walked down to the dining hall for supper
with a lighter tread. The pupils seemed disheartened, speaking in undertones, with none of the giggling and laughter
that usually accompanied mealtime. No doubt the funeral
still weighed heavily on their minds.

Meredith barely touched her pork pie and pickles, even
though it was one of her favorite meals. She kept feeling
she should do more for Kathleen, though nothing specific
came to mind.

Deciding to discuss it with the other teachers, she made
her way to the lounge, where Felicity and Essie had already claimed their seats by the window.

"We were wondering if you were going to join us," Felicity said, as Meredith sank onto a chair nearby. "I thought you might not feel up to it tonight."

Meredith smiled. "I would not miss our nightly discussions. As it happens, I have something to discuss with you." She looked up as the door opened.

Sylvia poked her head around the door. "May I join you?"

"Of course!" Essie cried, while Felicity scarcely lifted her head.

"Do come in." Meredith waved a hand at the empty chairs. "I was just about to have a discussion on what to do about commemorating Kathleen's work here."

Sylvia moved into the room and took a vacant chair. "I think that's a wonderful idea."

"Yes, it is." Felicity scowled at Sylvia as if she'd said something offensive.

Essie clasped her hands together. "Oh, what a lovely idea. What shall we do?"

"I was hoping you'd have some suggestions." Meredith looked from one to the other. "Anybody?"

"A plaque," Felicity said. "Brass plate on the outside wall where everyone can see it. Or in the hallway."

"I considered that." Meredith pondered for a moment or two. "I suppose it's the best thing."

"How about a memorial garden?" Sylvia suggested. "Just a small one, of course." She looked at Meredith. "You mentioned this afternoon that Miss Duncan was fond of flowers. We could have the pupils plant flowers in it each year, with some sort of ceremony. It would keep her memory alive for all the years to come."

Essie clapped her hands. "Yes, yes!"

"That's an outstanding idea!" Excited at the thought,

Meredith turned to Felicity. "What do you think of that, Felicity?"

She shrugged. "All right, I suppose. How would we get the plants to put in it?"

"Well, Tom would have to get them for us, of course." Meredith smiled at Sylvia. "Thank you, Miss Montrose. I'm sure Kathleen would like to know her work will be remembered in such a charming way."

Sylvia inclined her head. "My pleasure. And please, do call me Sylvia."

Felicity still look disgruntled, and her conversation lagged after that. Although she said nothing controversial, there was no mistaking the tension in the air. Even Essie failed to amuse her associates with her artless comments, and Meredith was quite relieved when Sylvia rose to leave.

"I am retiring for the night," she announced. "I will see you all in the morning."

The door had barely closed behind her when Felicity uttered a snort of disgust. "Such a hypocrite," she muttered. "Pretending to be so solicitous about someone she's never met." She screwed up her face and in a high lilting tone declared, " 'It would keep her memory alive for all the years to come.' "

"It is a good idea, though," Essie said timidly.

"Indeed it is." Meredith frowned at Felicity. "Much as Sylvia seems to annoy you, I'm afraid you will have to put up with her. She's here to take Kathleen's place, and we must do our best to make her welcome."

"She will never take Kathleen's place," Felicity muttered. "No one could."

"Maybe not, but she should at least have the opportunity to try." Meredith rose to her feet. "I suggest we all try to overlook her shortcomings and accept her into the fold. After all, let's not forget we are not exactly paragons of virtue ourselves."

"At least we are not afraid of progress and women's rights," Felicity said stoutly. "I can't abide a woman who refuses to recognize the blatant injustices committed against women—all women—since time began, and that it is well past time for change."

"All in good time." Meredith moved to the door. "Eventually all women will recognize the facts and take up the fight Until then, we have a mission here to undertake, and that is to see our young women leave this establishment with the skills to live a full life."

"In their husband's shadow," Felicity muttered.

"Never fear, Felicity. I'm quite sure that any young woman who has attended your class will have had the seeds of rebellion planted firmly in her mind. It will be up to each one of them what to make of it." With that, Meredith quietly closed the door.

On the way out of the hall she spied Amelia's room partner, Loretta, and managed to corner her in the quiet end of the corridor.

"Amelia tells me that you were with her when Miss Duncan brought her a book," Meredith said, as the girl stood fidgeting in front of her.

Loretta blinked, as if trying to remember. "Yes, miss, I was with her all night. We were studying together." She frowned. "Why? Is something wrong?"

"Ah, not at all, no. I was simply wondering if Miss Duncan happened to mention if she planned to meet someone on Saturday evening."

"No, miss. Not to us, she didn't."

Meredith glanced down the corridor to where a group of

girls stood quietly talking. "Do you happen to know if Penelope Fisher has returned to her room?"

Loretta shook her head. "I haven't seen her, miss."

"Well, that's all right. I'll find her later." Nodding and smiling, Meredith backed away, then turned and hurried down the hallway. The group of girls had broken up and most of them had wandered away by the time she reached them.

Her talk with Penelope would have to take place tomorrow, she decided. She'd had enough of questioning people for one day. In fact, she was sorely tempted to accept P.C. Shipham's verdict and let it rest at that.

She might even have done so had she not seen Kathleen's ghost again.

Feeling not in the least sleepy, she'd decided to take a walk around the school building for a breath of fresh air. Often the jaunt would relax her, and allow her to fall asleep.

She had just turned the corner and was proceeding along the back of the building when the familiar chill crept over her shoulders. She spun around and caught her breath. The cloud of mist hovered a few feet away, bathed in the pink glow of the late summer sunset.

Meredith darted a quick glance around her. The girls should all be in their rooms by now, preparing to retire for the night. She peered at the cloud, but could see nothing but the swirling mist. "Kathleen? Is that you?"

How ridiculous she sounded. Talking to a dead woman. Yet even as she began to back away, the face of Kathleen appeared in the center of the cloud.

Apprehension made Meredith's voice sharp. "Tell me what you want. Show me."

An arm appeared, and a hand. A finger pointed at

Meredith, then at the building behind her. She was about to speak when another arm appeared. For an instant she could see Kathleen quite clearly, arms raised above her head. Then the arms came down together, hard and fast, hands clasped.

Cold with shock, Meredith understood. Before she could speak, however, the apparition vanished, leaving her alone and shivering, in spite of the warm evening.

Meredith's restless sleep left her listless the next morning. When she joined the rest of the staff at breakfast, Felicity gave her an intense look that made her most uncomfortable.

"You don't seem well," she said, waving the piece of pork sausage on the end of her fork in Meredith's face, "This whole business of Kathleen is getting you down. Perhaps you should take a short respite. A day or two, perhaps. Essie and I can manage, now that Miss Montrose has joined us."

Her words were civil enough, but the irony in her tone was not lost on Sylvia, who sent her a disparaging glance from under her long lashes.

"I don't need a rest. I'm perfectly well." Meredith lifted her dainty cup from its saucer and sipped her tea.

"Well, you don't look it. Not still seeing ghosts, are you?"

Conscious of Sylvia's curious stare, Meredith put down her cup. "Have you tried these scones, Miss Montrose?" She reached for the plate and offered it to her. "Quite delicious. Our Mrs. Wilkins is an exceptional baker."

"I do believe I will try one." Sylvia took one of the scones and dropped it on her plate. "And again, please call me

Sylvia." She smiled at Meredith and Essie, while managing to avoid looking at Felicity. "It is so comforting to be on a first-name basis with everyone."

Felicity snorted, then turned it into a sneeze. Fishing a large man's handkerchief out of her sleeve, she loudly blew her nose. "Dratted hay fever," she muttered.

Fortunately, Sylvia chose to ignore the slight. She turned the conversation to the weather, and the rest of the meal passed in relative tranquillity.

Not that Meredith was feeling all that tranquil. The message Kathleen's ghost had given her was all too clear. Someone connected to the school was responsible for Kathleen's death. Of that she was quite sure.

Now she was all the more determined to find out the truth, without the help of anyone in authority. The reputation of the school depended on it. Somehow, she would have to convince Felicity and Essie of her convictions. She would need their help if she was to put this matter to rest.

Chapter 9

Meredith waited until the morning sessions were over before asking her friends to join her outside.

Felicity, as usual, rebelled against moving from the comfort of the teacher's lounge. "It has turned cool and cloudy out there," she said, leaning back in the comfortable chair. "I'm quite sure it's about to rain."

"I don't think so," Essie said timidly. "The clouds are much too high."

"I have something important I need to discuss with you both." Meredith glanced at the door as it opened. "Preferably alone."

Sylvia entered the room, looking flustered and out of sorts. "These young women are most unruly. I can't imagine any one of them successfully managing a houseful of servants. They are much too concerned with frivolities. They discuss the sort of gowns they will wear to their coming-out parties, or how they will wear their hair. They will be of no use to their future husbands if they don't start paying attention to the important aspects of a marriage."

Felicity's face was deceptively innocent as she inquired, "Such as?"

Sylvia rashly snatched at the bait. "Such as selecting the right furniture, suitable silverware, or hiring responsible servants, of course."

"I should think a more important aspect of a marriage is to procreate." Felicity rose from her chair. "I suggest we have a class to explain how that's done."

If she'd intended to shock Sylvia she certainly succeeded. The young woman's cheeks burned, and she tossed her head with a vindictive glare at the source of her discomfort. "I might have expected that sort of vulgar remark from you, Miss Cross. Then again, I suppose one should take into consideration and make allowances for your unfortunate background."

Meredith uttered a sound of protest, while Felicity strode across the room and shoved her nose up close to Sylvia's face. "You know nothing about my background," she snarled, "so I'll thank you to refrain from making deprecating remarks that have no substance whatsoever."

Sylvia took a step backward, though her triumphant expression made Meredith wonder uneasily just how much the woman did know about Felicity's past.

"Dratted woman," Felicity muttered, after Meredith had succeeded in ushering her and Essie into the hallway. "What do you suppose she knows about my background, anyway?"

"Probably nothing." Meredith glanced uneasily at her friend. "More than likely it was nothing but a wild shot in the dark."

"I'm not so sure. After all, it's in the school records that

I was in service for five years before you hired me. Easy enough for her to read it."

"Those records are private and locked in my desk. In any case, it is nothing to be ashamed of, considering you were forced into servitude after your father threw you out into the street, penniless and with nowhere to go."

Felicity snorted. "That monster. All because I wouldn't marry that ugly, fat crony of his. Not that I had any interest in marrying anyone after what my father did to me all those years. I swore when I left that no man would ever touch me again."

"I know." Meredith linked her arm through Felicity's and started leading her to the main doors. "I'm sorry that this business with Sylvia has brought up all those dreadful memories. Still, I can't believe she knows anything about your past. It's not a matter of public record."

"Maybe. But the fact that I served time in jail certainly is a matter of public record. Perhaps that's what she was referring to with that odious comment."

"Many women of high standing have served time in jail for protesting," Meredith reminded her. "Again, it is no cause for shame. It is the government who should be ashamed of incarcerating and torturing women for having the courage to stand up for what is right."

Felicity gave her a rare smile. "Well said, sister. I couldn't agree more."

Essie, who had followed them silently down the corridor, spoke up. "It is nobody's business what has taken place in someone's past. That is a personal issue, and should not be a matter of record at all."

"Yes, well, not all of us have your pristine background." Felicity reached the door ahead of them all and dragged it open. "Be thankful you have nothing to hide." Fortunately, she barged out the door in her usual rambunctious manner and missed Essie's expression.

Meredith couldn't help wondering what Felicity would say had she known that Essie had demons of her own to hide, and that apart from those directly involved in the scandal, the sordid facts were known only to Meredith.

She had no time to ponder the question, since the moment she stepped out into the fresh air Felicity pounced on her.

"Now pray tell us why you have asked us out under these gray skies when the bell will ring any minute to summon us to the dining hall."

"It is a little chilly out here." Essie pulled her lacy shawl closer about her shoulders. She looked a little pale, though Meredith was inclined to believe Felicity's unintentional mention of her past was the cause of her discomfort.

"I wanted to talk to you about Kathleen," Meredith announced, when she considered they had walked far enough from the steps to avoid being overheard.

"About the memorial garden?" Felicity nodded. "I suppose we should decide where we're going to put it. Have you talked to Tom about getting the plants? He'll have to dig the flower beds, of course. Better to get Davie to do that. Have you decided where to put it? Somewhere in the woods, I should think, where it's sheltered. I—"

"Felicity." Meredith halted and stood in front of her. "I want to talk about Kathleen's murder."

Felicity frowned, while Essie uttered a little moan of dismay.

"Kathleen is dead and buried," Felicity said sharply. "Let her rest in peace, Meredith, for heaven's sake."

"That's exactly my point." Meredith glanced over her

shoulder to make sure no one was about. "Kathleen is not at peace. Nor will she be, until her murderer is apprehended."

"I don't see how we can do anything about that. Whoever killed her has long ago made his escape and could be anywhere by now."

"I don't think so. In fact, I'm quite sure that whoever killed Kathleen is still somewhere on these grounds and is, in fact, someone connected to the school."

Essie whimpered, her hand covering her mouth, while Felicity shook her head. "Bosh, Meredith. You really must get rid of these fanciful ideas—"

"They are not fanciful, Felicity." Meredith folded her arms in defiance. "Someone connected to this school killed Kathleen and everyone here is in danger until we find out who did this dreadful deed and why. The fact that I can see Kathleen's ghost and you can't doesn't alter the facts. We must uncover the killer's identity as quickly as we possibly can, or there might very well be another tragedy committed on the grounds of Bellehaven."

"Then why don't you ask Kathleen who killed her, since you appear to have this remarkable ability to converse with her?"

Meredith sighed. "I didn't say I could converse with her. I can barely see her. She fades in and out like the moon passing between the clouds. All I can do is watch her signals and try to interpret them."

Felicity's expression was of pure skepticism. "What kind of signals?"

For answer, Meredith pointed at the building, then clasped her hands and brought them down hard, as Kathleen had done.

Essie uttered a squeak of dismay, while Felicity's face remained impassive. A long pause followed, while she appeared to struggle with conflicting thoughts.

"Very well," she said finally. "I'm still not convinced, but obviously you feel strongly enough about this to believe you saw Kathleen's ghost. Since I doubt that we shall have any peace until this matter is resolved, I will endeavor to help you find Kathleen's killer."

"Thank you." Thrilled with her victory, Meredith turned to Essie. "I'll understand if you would prefer not to participate in this venture. Your nerves are not strong, and this could be quite an ordeal for you."

Essie's eyes stared back at her, full of fear and uncertainty. "I am more afraid of a killer being allowed to run loose among us. I should like to help in anyway that I can to see him locked away where he cannot harm any more of us."

"Then it's settled." Meredith smiled at her friends in satisfaction. "We are officially on the trail of Kathleen's killer." She turned toward the flower beds, though no cloud hovered there that she could see. "Never fear, Kathleen. We will find him, so that you may rest in peace at last."

"Amen," Essie said softly.

A moment later Felicity muttered, "Oh, all right. Amen from me, too."

Meredith felt another surge of triumph. She had won the support of her dear friends, and she was certain now that Kathleen's killer would be brought to justice. After all, three heads were better than one, were they not?

"So where do we start?" Felicity demanded, as the three of them walked back into the school. "Do you have any idea where to begin looking for this nefarious monster?"

"Not much, I'm afraid," Meredith admitted. "I have a

vague idea that the flower beds are involved, since Kathleen chooses to appear there, and she keeps pointing at the flowers, though I must confess, I don't know why."

Felicity sniffed. "Not a terrible lot to go on, is it."

"Perhaps it has something to do with Tom," Essie offered.

Felicity sniffed again—loud enough to be a snort this time. "Tom wouldn't have the strength to lift that branch, much less bash Kathleen over the head with it."

Essie whimpered, and Felicity turned on her. "If you insist on making that noise every time one of us mentions the murder, you'll be more hindrance than help."

"I'm sorry." Essie's lower lip trembled. "I just don't have the stomach for all this violence. Perhaps I should stay out of your way after all."

"Nonsense." Felicity took her arm and pulled her toward the dining hall. "This is a golden opportunity for you to acquire a tougher constitution. By the time we have solved this dilemma, you will no doubt find yourself a much sturdier person, and be the better for it."

Meredith had a few qualms on that score, but said nothing. She knew how badly Essie wanted to be accepted as an equal, and her constant struggle to attain that was sometimes agonizing to see.

Essie, however, had to make her own way and conquer her fears. The best way to achieve that was to include her, even if the venture might prove daunting. No one knew that better than Felicity. She had faced and conquered her own fears, and knew the rewards. Then again, she was made of much sterner stuff. Meredith could only hope Essie survived whatever might lay in store for them, without losing her mind altogether.

The teachers separated during the main midday meals,

each taking a table to supervise the young ladies and hope-fully teach them manners.

On this day Meredith happened to be seated close to the tomboy Penelope Fisher, and seized the opportunity to speak with her as everyone was dismissed from the table.

"Someone mentioned they saw you crying last Saturday evening," she said, as the young girl filed past her. "I do hope it wasn't anything serious. Did someone upset you?"

The girl looked about to burst into tears right then and there. "Yes, Mrs. Llewellyn. There's been a death in my family," she said, her voice breaking. "My mother sent me a letter to tell me Grandmama had passed away."

"Oh, I'm so sorry." Frustrated at yet another end to the trail, Meredith nevertheless felt a deep sympathy for the child. "I imagine you would like leave to go to the funeral."

Tears spilled down the girl's cheeks. "I would dearly love to go. My parents will not allow me to attend. They say it is important I finish my studies here."

"I'm so sorry." Meredith touched the young girl's arm. "I can imagine what a disappointment that must be."

Penelope muttered her thanks and slipped away.

As Meredith was about to follow her, she caught sight of Amelia Webster among a group of young women filing toward the door. The girl sharply turned her head, but Mere-dith had no doubt she had been watching her exchange with Penelope. Idle curiosity, no doubt.

She forgot Amelia as Felicity drew her aside the minute she stepped out into the hallway. "I've been thinking," she said. "When Essie suggested Kathleen's killer might be the gardener I dismissed it at once, but it occurred to me later that perhaps that assistant of his had something to do with it. Never did like that lad. Very shifty if you ask me."

"He's shy, that's all," Meredith murmured.

"Well, it wouldn't hurt to find out where he was on Saturday night."

Meredith didn't answer. She was thinking about the last time she saw Davie, slinking away through the trees, sobbing. Perhaps it would be a good idea to have a word with him.

Just then she heard her name called, and looked up to see Sylvia hurrying toward them.

"Here comes Miss Nuisance," Felicity muttered. "Wonder what bee she has in her bonnet now."

Meredith had no chance to respond as Sylvia reached them, her face flushed from exertion. "I've been looking all over for you, Meredith," she said breathlessly. "One of the drawers in my desk is locked and there doesn't appear to be a key to it anywhere."

Meredith frowned. "It wasn't like Kathleen to lock her drawers. There must be a key to her desk somewhere. I'll have Mrs. Wilkins look for it."

"Thank you. I'd appreciate that." Acting as if Felicity was invisible, she sped off, leaving Meredith to deal with her friend's righteous indignation.

"Did you see that?" Felicity stared after the flying figure in disgust. "Totally ignored me, as if I were no more than a mere speck of dust."

"She did seem to be in rather a hurry." Meredith sighed. "I suppose I'll have to ask Mrs. Wilkins to search for the missing key. Though it could be anywhere. All of Kathleen's personal property has been sent on to her family. The key to her desk could well have gone with it."

"Well, there's no need to worry. I can open the dratted drawer for Miss Prissy."

Meredith glanced at Felicity in concern. "You're not thinking of attacking it with a hammer, I trust?"

"Good Lord, no. I leave those kind of tactics to Reggie. He loves to beat the blazes out of everything. It was his handiwork that caused the water pipe to leak. The brace had come loose and instead of screwing the bracket back in place he wacked it with a sledgehammer. Put a split right around the pipe, the fool."

"Oh, dear. Well, I wouldn't want to damage the drawer. Perhaps we can get a locksmith to open it."

A group of students drifted toward them and Felicity leaned closer, lowering her voice. "If Kathleen locked that drawer, there must be something in it she didn't want anyone to see. Am I right?"

"Perhaps, but—"

"Then we need to open it ourselves, when no one else is around." She clicked her tongue. "Don't look at me like that, Meredith. I can open that drawer and no one will ever know I've touched it."

Meredith widened her eyes. "How—"

"Don't ask." Felicity paused, waiting for the students to pass before whispering fiercely, "My time in prison wasn't totally wasted, you know. I picked up some interesting skills while I was in there." She pulled back. "They come in handy at times."

"Indeed." Meredith smiled. "I can't wait to find out what other talents you acquired."

Felicity grunted, but the look on her face closely resembled that of a cat having stolen a tasty morsel from the dinner table. She started down the corridor, and Meredith hurried after her. They would have to wait until the close of classes that afternoon, but now she couldn't wait to find out what Kathleen had hidden away from prying eyes.

Although it was unlikely, she couldn't help wondering if the drawer might contain a clue as to what Kathleen was doing that last evening of her life. A clue that could possibly lead her to the identity of Kathleen's killer.

As it was, she had to wait until after supper to satisfy her curiosity. Felicity had chosen to stay late in her classroom to help a pupil understand the meaning of Thomas Gray's immortal "Elegy."

Throughout the meal Meredith's impatience held her appetite at bay, and she was quite unable to enjoy the shepherd's pie Mrs. Wilkins had so expertly prepared. As she was struggling to finish her pear crumble pudding, Felicity rose from her seat across the hall and approached her table.

"I'll meet you outside Kathleen's room," she muttered, her words masked by the hum of chatter from the pupils.

Meredith laid down her spoon and fork. "Ladies!" She waited until she had the attention of everyone at the table. "I have an urgent appointment to attend. As soon as you are finished with your meal, you may leave the table."

She stood up, conscious of the curious glances directed at her. Normally she waited until the last girl had been excused from the table before leaving herself.

Hurrying to the door, she wasn't sure if she was anxious to find out what was in Kathleen's desk, or simply eager to watch Felicity apply the doubtful skills she'd learned in prison.

Chapter 10

Meredith could see no sign of Felicity in the corridor, and she hurried to Kathleen's room, determined not to miss the remarkable feat.

Upon opening the door she saw her friend at Kathleen's desk, tugging each drawer open until one refused to budge. "Ah," she muttered. "Here we go."

Meredith quickly closed the door and sped over to the desk. "Do let me watch."

"Come around here then." Felicity reached up to her head and pulled a long hairpin from her auburn coils. She straightened out the thin wire, then slightly curved one end. Bending almost double, she peered closely at the lock and poked the pin into it.

After jiggling it around for moment or two, she grunted in triumph. "This should do it." She gave the pin a sharp tug, then pulled on the drawer. It slid smoothly open.

"Well!" Meredith stared at the open drawer. "I don't know whether to be impressed by your expertise or appalled that you are so adept at such a disreputable practice."

Felicity grinned. "I must admit, it has come in useful at times."

Meredith uttered a shocked gasp. "Don't tell me you have done this before?"

"Of course I shan't tell you. These matters are delicate and should not be discussed, even among friends."

Unsure if her friend was merely teasing, Meredith decided to ignore the comment. "Well, let's see what Kathleen was hiding in her drawer, shall we?" She drew out a sheaf of papers, which appeared to be test scores from the week before. Disappointed, she laid them on the desk. "We must see that Sylvia is given these."

"I still can't think of this desk belonging to that scatter-brained woman." Felicity gazed at the clean blackboard, her expression remote. "It will always be Kathleen's desk to me, and Kathleen's room. No matter who might occupy it in the future."

"In time we shall get used to it," Meredith said gently. She was about to close the drawer when she spied the corner of a slip of paper tucked away in the back. "Wait a minute." She drew it out. "What's this?"

She started to read the scrawled words on the note, which was of the very best quality paper and had a crest embossed at the top of the page. As the meaning became clear, she gasped in horror.

Felicity leaned in to read it out loud over Meredith's shoulder. "Dearest Deirdre, I can hardly bear to wait until I can hold you in my arms again. I shall be waiting at our usual rendezvous tonight. Please don't keep me waiting too long, my precious."

Felicity's voice had grown more strained with each

word, and now she could barely get out the last words. "Your Victor."

Stunned, Meredith studied the crest with the large S inside it. "Silkwood," she murmured. "Of course, so that's who it was."

Felicity stared at her. "Are you saying that Victor Silkwood is meeting with one of our pupils? But that's outrageous! Apart from the fact that the man has a wife, he's at least twenty years older than any of our girls."

"Deirdre Lamont," Meredith said, still staring at the incriminating words. "Olivia saw Mr. Silkwood arguing with one of our pupils in Witcheston the other day. I asked her about it and she described the girl. At the time her description could have fit several of our pupils, but now I realize it had to be Deirdre Lamont."

Felicity sniffed. "Well, I can't say I'm utterly astounded. That girl is far too brazen for her own good. I blame that contemptible man, however. He should know better. Why is it that some men think that having a certain social standing allows them to behave in a way that resembles animals in heat?"

Meredith choked. "Let us hope it has not progressed that far. It's obvious Kathleen has had a word with Deirdre. She must have confiscated the note from her, possibly while Deirdre was trying to pass it on to someone else to read." She pointed to the words at the foot of the notepaper in Kathleen's neat handwriting. *Speak to her parents.*

"Apparently she never had time to talk to Deirdre's parents before she died. We shall have to contact them ourselves."

"I'll have a word with Deirdre first," Meredith said quickly. "It may not be necessary to bring her parents into this."

"Well, that I shall leave up to you." Felicity stuck the hairpin back into her hair. "But I tell you, I should love to give that disgusting Mr. Silkwood a piece of my mind."

"I heartily agree. That will not help Deirdre, however, and will only make things more difficult for us, since he is such a prominent member of the board."

"Drat it, Meredith! Can't you use your charm on Stuart Hamilton and have that slimy snake removed? If you tell Hamilton what's been going on——"

"He will more likely remove Deirdre than Mr. Silkwood. You know how these men stick together."

"Yes, I do. Like cow dung to your shoe."

In spite of her concern, Meredith sputtered with laughter. "I don't think Mr. Hamilton would appreciate that."

"Mr. Hamilton fails to appreciate a lot of things."

"Well, he's a busy man."

Felicity grunted her disapproval. "Well, I sincerely hope that whatever Kathleen said to Deirdre, it was dire enough to put an end to her relationship with that despicable rake."

"I suppose that is something I shall have to find out." Meredith did not relish the thought of talking to the young lady about such a delicate subject. She decided it might be better to put it off until the morning, when she would have a fresher mind to deal with it.

As it was, first thing the following morning Tom hailed her as she was crossing the lobby on her way to morning assembly.

"Young Davie didn't turn up for work this mornin'," he told her, twisting his panama into a tight roll between his gnarled hands. "He weeded them flower beds like you asked. I noticed last night they need attending again. I was going to clip his ear this mornin' as a reminder, but he ain't here."

"He's most likely overslept." Already late, Meredith backed away. "I wouldn't concern yourself too much."

Tom shook his head. "No, m'm, I don't think that's it. Davie's mum always gets him out of bed at the proper time. Real stickler, she is, about him getting here on time."

The increasing murmur of voices down the hallway warned Meredith the students were getting impatient. "I'm sorry, Tom, but I'm in a rush. If Davie isn't here by the time assembly is over, please let me know."

Tom's shoulders sagged. "Yes, m'm. I'll be sure 'n do that."

"Also, I need to talk to you about something else just as soon as I am free." Meredith hesitated for an instant, and then sped down the hallway to the assembly hall. Whatever the problem was with Davie, it would have to wait.

She had barely begun her morning address when the first niggling worry surfaced. Davie might be withdrawn and oversensitive but he was usually reliable. What if something had happened to him, too? What if he'd seen something he shouldn't have seen and had to be done away with, so to speak?

The more she thought about it, the more convinced she became that something dreadful had happened to poor Davie. The moment assembly was concluded she rushed out of the hall without so much as a word of explanation.

She would have to placate Felicity later, she told herself, remembering that lady's shocked expression as she'd flown past her. Right now, however, it was imperative that she speak with Tom again.

She found him in the flower beds, pulling the new weeds. A light drizzle had begun pattering on the leaves and blossoms of the foxgloves and lupins, dampening the soil. The enhanced fragrance reminded Meredith sharply of Kathleen, and she half expected to see her misty shape forming beneath the trees.

Tom straightened as she approached, and she concentrated on the matter at hand. "Has Davie arrived yet?" she asked him, and was dismayed when he shook his head.

Removing his hat, he muttered, "I don't know what's got into the lad lately, m'm. Honest I don't. Used to be a good worker, he did, but ever since we found Miss Duncan lying dead like that, our Davie has been in a thick fog. Don't hear a word I say to him, and he don't seem to know whether he's coming or going these days."

It was a long speech for Tom, and Meredith nodded sympathetically throughout, barely able to contain her impatience until Tom had finished speaking. "I should like the carriage made ready," she said, when Tom finally paused for breath. "Tell Reggie to have it at the front gate in half an hour."

Tom looked surprised, as well he might. The ladies rarely left the school building, except to walk to church or into the village. Using the carriage was reserved for the most special of occasions. "Going into town, m'm?"

Meredith hesitated, reluctant to alarm the gardener unnecessarily.

He must have taken it as a silent rebuke, as he dipped his head and mumbled, "Sorry, m'm. None of my business, I'm sure. I'll go and tell Reggie to get the carriage ready."

"It's all right, Tom. I just want to pay a visit to Davie's house, and it's a little far for me to walk. I don't want to be away for too long, since I have a class in an hour."

Tom's weathered face crinkled in dismay. "You think there's trouble for our Davie? Per'aps I should come with you, m'm. Don't like to think of you going alone."

"That's quite all right." Meredith waved a hand at the

flower beds. "I'd rather you see to these weeds. Miss Duncan won't be happy until they are all gone."

Seeing Tom's puzzled stare, she realized too late how ridiculous that sounded. She uttered a light laugh. "Do listen to me. I'm afraid I'm having trouble believing she's gone from us. I keep forgetting she isn't here to scold us for neglecting her precious flower beds."

"I reckon Davie is happy about that much, m'm," Tom said, digging his hoe into the soft soil. "Took it hard, he did, when she shouted at him."

Meredith mulled over his words as she hurried back to the building. It seemed odd that Davie was in the vicinity on at least two occasions when Kathleen had made her appearance. She could still hear his pitiful sobbing among the trees.

Kathleen had seemed agitated on both those occasions. Meredith slowed her step. Could it be possible that Kathleen had been pointing, not at the flowers in the flower beds, but at Davie standing a few feet away? Was Kathleen trying to tell her that the young lad, reacting in anger at being scolded, had slammed that tree limb at her head?

If so, then Meredith had more than one question to ask when she got to Davie's house.

Olivia heaved the carpet sweeper up the stairs, banging it against the bannisters with intensifying fury. "Two weeks without a day off. That miserable cow. It should have been her what got bashed over the head, not Miss Duncan. What bloody right does Mona have, taking away our time off?"

Grace trailed up the stairs behind her, a bucket in one

hand and mop in the other. How she hated it when Olivia got into one of her snits. It usually ended up in trouble for both of them, and they were in enough trouble right now as it was. "I s'pose it could have been worse," she said, hoping to soothe her friend's temper.

Olivia reached the top of the stairs and turned on her. "How could it be worse? How is anything worse than being stuck in this rotten building day after day for two whole weeks? I'll miss buying me magazine and sweets in the village. You know how I get when I don't get sweets to eat."

"You could always steal some sugar from the bin." Grace started walking down the corridor to the windows at the end. "It's better than nothing."

Olivia slammed the sweeper down on the carpet, jarring the fragile base so that it rattled. "I'll tell you what's better than nothing. Getting even with that sourpuss Mona, that's what."

Grace spun around in alarm. "Olivia Bunting! Don't you dare! You could lose us our jobs."

"Nah. They'd never get maids to work out here in the middle of nowhere, with only a bunch of toffee-nosed debs for company. In any case, we'd have more fun working in the village. We'd at least see some blokes now and then."

"I thought you was off blokes." Grace turned back. "Isn't that why we went protesting and got into trouble in the first place?"

"That's different. That's not messing up me personal life. I was just getting to know that new bloke at the ironmonger's in the High Street and now some other floozie's going to get his attention and he'll forget all about me."

"No he won't." Grace laughed. "How could he forget

you falling over your own two feet walking in the door the other day?"

"I didn't see the coal scuttle stuck out there, did I." Olivia rattled the sweeper some more. "Anyhow, I'm going to get back at Moaning Minnie, so there."

Thoroughly unnerved now, Grace carefully lowered the bucket of hot water. Still clinging to her mop, she faced her friend. "How are you going to do that, then?"

"I don't know." Olivia kicked the toe of her black oxford shoe against the sweeper's nose. "I'll think of something, though." She shifted her glance to the bucket of water.

Grace's dread thickened as she watched a wicked smile cross over the other girl's face.

"I know," Olivia murmured. She grinned and rubbed her hands together. "I know exactly what I'm going to do. Mona won't even see it coming."

Grace whimpered. "Oh, no, Livvy. Please, don't. She'll know it was you and we'll both be chucked out of here. I know it."

Olivia shook her head. "The debs are always playing tricks on her. I heard that someone tied Mona's shoelaces together once and she fell flat on her face. Wish I could have seen that."

"I don't like, it, Livvy. She'll know it was us, I tell you."

"Nah." Olivia shook her head. "She'll never know for sure who did it."

"Did what?"

"Wait and see. It'll be good, that's all I'm going to tell you for now."

She started shoving the sweeper back and forth over the carpet, its wheels squeaking so loudly Grace couldn't even think. She didn't want any part of whatever Olivia had planned, but somehow she knew no matter what she did, she'd share the blame for whatever happened to Mona, and this time they'd lose a lot more than days off.

Normally Meredith enjoyed a ride in the carriage. She found it most pleasant to sit back and watch the countryside roll past her without any effort on her part. She liked listening to the jingling of the harness and the clatter of Major's hooves on the hard surface of the road.

The poor horse didn't get out much, and was beginning to get a middle-aged spread around his belly. That might have concerned her on a normal day, but this morning she sat with her shoulders hunched and her jaw clenched as the carriage rattled along the twisting lanes that led to Davie's house.

In her rush to get there, she had completely forgotten to mention the memorial garden to Tom. That would have to wait now until she'd taken care of this business with his assistant.

Davie's father would no doubt be tending to his farm, but Meredith hoped Davie's mother would be at home and able to set her mind at rest about the young lad.

The moment Reggie halted Major in front of the farmhouse, Meredith opened the door and climbed down.

Reggie jumped down from his seat at the same time and frowned at her. "I would have given you a hand, m'm, if you'd waited a moment."

"That's all right, Reggie. I shan't be but a minute or two. Would you please lead Major over there to that patch of grass where he can graze." She pointed to a patch of thick grass across the road."

"Very well, m'm." Looking somewhat disgruntled, Reggie led Major over to the other side of the road.

Paying him no attention, Meredith opened the gate and walked up the path, her feet crunching on the gravel.

Mrs. Gray must have heard her coming, as the front door opened the minute Meredith reached the step.

"Mrs. Llewellyn!" the farmer's wife exclaimed. "How nice of you to call."

Meredith hesitated. If something terrible had happened to Davie, his mother might not yet be aware of it. On the other hand, if he was responsible for Kathleen's death, it would all come out sooner or later. There seemed nothing for it but to bring up the subject immediately. "I've come to inquire about Davie," she said, wondering how on earth she was going to phrase the questions she needed to ask.

"Oh, that's very kind of you, m'm." Mrs. Gray pulled the door open wider. "Won't you please come in? I'll pop a kettle on the hob for a nice cup of tea."

Nodding in agreement, Meredith stepped into the cozy parlor. The smell of bread baking made her mouth water, and it was with some effort that she said, "Thank you, Mrs. Gary, but I'm afraid I don't have time for tea. We were wondering why Davie didn't come in to work today. Tom is quite concerned about him."

Mrs. Gray's expression changed to bewilderment. "Didn't you get the message I sent with Jim? He was supposed to leave a message when he dropped off the milk at your school this morning."

Meredith frowned. "Really? I wonder who got the message. Tom didn't hear it and I certainly didn't." She glanced out the window to where Reggie was standing next to the carriage, hands in his pockets, his lips pursed in a whistle. "I'll have to make some inquiries," she added grimly. "I do hope there's nothing seriously amiss with Davie?"

"Nothing a day or two in bed won't cure." Mrs. Gray

ran a nervous hand over her bound hair. "Davie's stomach is giving him trouble, that's all. He's been really upset ever since that Miss Duncan died. Hasn't been eating properly, that's the trouble. He thought a lot of her, our Davie."

"As did we all." Meredith hesitated. "Did Davie happen to go out at all last Saturday night?"

Mrs. Gray looked puzzled. "Go out?"

"I was just wondering if he happened to be at the school. We're trying to piece together what actually happened to Miss Duncan and it would be helpful if someone had seen something that might help."

Davie's mother shook her head. "Davie was home here at five o'clock, just like he is every night. He spent the evening helping his dad mend a cart wheel."

"He didn't go out after that?"

"No, m'm, he didn't. I can say that for sure." She leaned forward a little and whispered, "I don't like telling people this, but our Davie walks in his sleep. I had a lock put on his door and I lock him in at night. Afraid he'll fall down the stairs and hurt himself, I am."

"Ah." Meredith smiled. "Don't worry, Mrs. Gray. I shan't say a word about it to anyone. Just tell Davie to come back when he's feeling better."

"Oh, he'll be back tomorrow, Mrs. Llewellyn. I'm sure of it." She glanced across the room to a door on the other side. "Are you sure you won't stop for a spot of tea?"

"Thank you, no. I must get back to my class." Meredith headed for the door. "But I do appreciate the offer."

"Not at all, m'm. It's a pleasure to see you." The farmer's wife opened the door. "And I hope they catch whoever hit that poor Miss Duncan over the head, indeed I do. Nasty bit of work, whoever did that."

Meredith tried not to show her concern as she bid the

woman good-bye. It seemed as if word had spread outside the school that Kathleen's death was no accident. At least it appeared that Davie had nothing to do with it, which greatly relieved her.

But now she was back to the big question again. Who had killed Kathleen, and why?

Deep in thought, she hardly noticed the passing scenery on the way back, and was surprised when Reggie halted Major in front of the school gates.

She left him to stable the horse and hurried up the driveway to the school. The jangling of the bell signaling the commencement of classes echoed through the corridors as she headed for her classroom.

Thirteen pairs of eyes followed her all the way to her desk. Accustomed to seeing her waiting in her chair when they filed into the room, her pupils no doubt were wondering what on earth had possessed her that morning. First she'd dashed off before breakfast was over and now here she was, tearing into the classroom at the very last minute instead of waiting sedately at her desk.

Still sorely out of breath, she barely managed a greeting before turning to the blackboard. The subject for that class was a study of the works of Emile Munier, and she began to write his name. Halfway through his surname the chalk broke, resulting in a jagged smear instead of neat letters. Someone behind her giggled, and she turned sharply to utter a rebuke.

The words never left her mouth. Standing by the window, as clear as day, hovered the ghostly figure of Kathleen.

Chapter 11

"You've got to help me," Olivia said, as she shoved the carpet sweeper back in the cupboard. "I can't do it all by meself."

"I'm not going to help you do nothing," Grace declared. She wrung out the mop and squeezed it in next to the sweeper. "I'm going to stay out of it."

"Are we friends or not?" Olivia dug her hands into her hips and glared at her.

Grace swallowed. She could sense that she was being backed into a corner and knowing Olivia, she'd get her way. Angry at herself for being such a softie, she muttered, "You know we're friends."

"Then why won't you help me?"

"Because you'll get us into big trouble, that's why."

"No I won't. Mona will never know it was us. She'll think it were that Loretta and that roommate of hers. They're always playing pranks on people, them two."

"What if she does find out it's us?"

"She won't." Olivia grabbed her by the arm. "Come on. She'll be doing her rounds by now. We can sneak into her room with the bucket—"

Grace halted, dragging Olivia to a stop. "What bucket? What are you going to do?"

Olivia grinned. "Fill it with water and balance it over the door. Then when Moaning Minnie pushes the door open, the bucket overturns and pours the water . . . all . . . over . . . her." She'd spluttered out the last words through gusts of laughter.

Grace wasn't laughing. "You're off your flippin' rocker, you are."

Olivia shook her head, still giggling. "No, really. I saw it in a film down at the cinema. These two blokes did it to another bloke. You should have seen him. Soaking wet, he was . . ." She broke into another bout of laughing.

"I'm not going to do it." Grace pulled her arm free and started marching down the hallway to the kitchen.

"Spoilsport. Scaredy-cat!" Olivia danced behind her. "I'll get Reggie to help me, then. He'll do it if I promise to give him a kiss."

Shocked, Grace halted once more. "You wouldn't!"

"I'll have to if you won't help me."

Torn between her fear of reprisal and her loyalty to her friend, Grace wavered, then said weakly, "All right, I'll help. But don't blame me if we both end up in the work-house."

Olivia rushed over to her and hugged her. "I knew you was really my friend. Come on. I'll get the bucket and you bring a chair. We'll need one to stand on."

Grace followed her to the kitchen, her heart hammering so hard she thought it would explode inside her chest. Every instinct told her she was making a terrible mistake, but she couldn't seem to help herself. When Olivia said jump, she jumped.

One of these days, she promised herself, she'd learn to stand up to her friend and say no. For the time being, however, it looked very much as if she'd be involved in yet another of Olivia's disasters. She didn't even want to think about what might happen if they were caught. It would be lights out for both of them, that was for sure.

For several seconds Meredith could do nothing but stare at the misty outline of Kathleen's ghost. She stared so long that several of the young women turned their heads to see what she was looking at so intently.

Fully expecting screams to erupt, Meredith braced herself. Instead, the girls looked back at her as if she'd gone completely out of her mind.

It took her several more seconds to realize that they couldn't see what she could see. Kathleen's image still hovered there, so clearly she could see the expression on her late friend's face. She could think of only one word to describe it. Desperation.

Even so, it was apparent that she was the only one in the room who could actually see the apparition, since by now everyone in the entire class had looked over her shoulder to see what all the fuss was about.

Meredith cleared her throat. "I was hoping that the rain had stopped," she said, waving her hand in the general direction of Kathleen's ghost. "I thought we . . . er . . . might all go outside to study . . . ah . . . the still life that was so . . . uh . . . prominent in the works of Manet and Cézanne."

The response to her stuttering announcement brought only blank stares. Trying valiantly to ignore the ghostly figure by the windows, Meredith fixed her eye on a student in the front row. "We will . . . er . . . select some items to bring back to class, such as . . . um . . . ferns, twigs, flowers—"

She broke off abruptly as Kathleen's transparent arms lifted up and down in a sort of languid frenzy. There she goes again, Meredith thought, with just an edge of irritation. The very mention of flowers seemed to throw Kathleen into a dither.

She frowned at the ghost and shook her head. Really, this was all becoming quite a distraction.

Still glaring in the direction of the windows, she said firmly, "Since it is still raining, however, that will have to wait for another day. In the meantime, we will study the life and works of Emile Munier."

She turned her back on the windows and carefully finished writing the name on the blackboard. Facing the class again, she began, "Munier was born in Paris on June 2, 1840. He—"

She broke off again as a sharp movement from the windows caught her eye. Kathleen was pointing, or rather more like jabbing a finger, at the group of students seated in front of her.

Meredith followed the gesture, but it was so vague she couldn't pinpoint the target of Kathleen's urgent signals. Frustrated, she looked back at the ghost. "What is it you're trying to tell me?"

Kathleen threw her arms out in an expansive arc, then faded rapidly into a mere wisp of smoke. In the next breath, she'd disappeared entirely.

A rustle of whispers among the girls called Meredith's attention back to her duties. Only then did she realize she'd spoken out loud. She cleared her throat, took a firmer grip on the piece of chalk, and turned back to the blackboard.

Puzzling out what Kathleen wanted so badly to tell her would have to wait until she was no longer in full view of thirteen very curious young ladies.

Somehow she managed to get through the rest of the class, though she couldn't resist an occasional peek at the windows whenever the students had their heads down.

Kathleen failed to reappear, however, though Meredith was far from reassured. If the ghost intended to make a habit of popping up all over the place willy-nilly, Meredith would have to make it quite clear that she did not appreciate the distraction.

Though how she would convey that, while apparently unable to communicate on any viable level, was quite the mystery. Somehow she would have to find a way to interpret Kathleen's signals, vague as they were, and set the poor woman's mind at rest. Perhaps then she could continue on her journey and leave everyone else in peace.

With a huge sense of relief Meredith heard the end-of-session bell ring, and was at last free to dismiss her class. She would not have another until that afternoon, which would give her some time to ponder on the enigma in which her late friend had her embroiled.

The pupils sedately filed past her to the door, each of them sending her a sideways glance as if worried she might suddenly throw a fit, or something equally upsetting. She made herself smile at each one, hoping to reassure them that she was not about to lose her mind.

A slim girl with dark brown hair sauntered past, jogging Meredith's memory. She had almost forgotten she needed to have a word with Deirdre Lamont. Hastily she called out after her.

"Deirdre, I'd like to see you in my office right away, if you please."

Deirdre stopped, turning a sulky face toward her. "I'm supposed to go to Miss Montrose's class next."

"Not for another fifteen minutes. What I have to say won't take that long. Run along now. I'll join you in a minute."

For a second or two it seemed that Deirdre would argue, but then she raised her shoulders in an unbecoming shrug and stalked out the door.

Anticipating a difficult encounter with the young woman, Meredith sighed as she followed several paces behind her down the corridor. How she hated interfering in someone's personal business. Unfortunately, she had no choice in the matter. As long as Deirdre resided at the school, Meredith was responsible for her well-being, and illicit assignations with a married man definitely did not bode well for the young woman's welfare.

She reached the door of her office, where Deirdre stood waiting, her hands clasped defiantly behind her back. Ushering her inside, Meredith closed the door and seated herself behind her desk.

Wasting no time, she said quietly, "It has come to my attention that you have been carrying on an association of sorts with a certain gentleman in the village, who is not only considerably advanced in age but happens to have a wife and family. I'm sure I don't have to point out that this is not a healthy relationship and will have to cease immediately."

Deirdre's cheeks turned a dull red, but her eyes sparked with defiance. "Pardon me for saying so, Mrs. Llewellyn, but what I do outside the school is my own business."

"Not entirely, considering the fact you played truant in order to meet this person." Meredith leaned forward. "Your parents have entrusted me with your welfare while you are under my supervision. That includes any activities you may care to indulge in outside the school grounds, if it affects said welfare."

Deirdre tossed her head. "I don't know why you're picking on me, miss. I'm not the only one sneaking out to meet a secret boyfriend."

Meredith frowned. "Who else, may I ask, is conducting themselves in this disgraceful manner?"

"It's not my place to say."

Hesitating, Meredith decided that was a matter best pursued later. "Well, in any case, what other girls do doesn't excuse you, or allow you to continue with this unfortunate arrangement. You will either give me your word you will not meet with Mr. Silkwood again, or I shall hand the matter over to your parents. Is that understood?"

The threat of talking to her parents succeeded in penetrating Deirdre's wall of rebellion. Her hand strayed to the gaudy enameled butterfly brooch she had pinned to the high lace collar at her throat. Lowering her gaze, she muttered, "Yes, Mrs. Llewellyn."

"I have your word?"

"Yes, Mrs. Llewellyn."

Satisfied, Meredith nodded. "Then you may leave."

Without looking up, Deirdre turned and marched to the door.

Meredith waited until the door had closed behind her before letting out her breath. How unpleasant! She hoped she wouldn't have to do that again. She gave a fleeting thought to the other girl Deirdre had mentioned, then dismissed it. More than likely Deirdre had made the whole thing up as a defense for her own actions.

In any case, Meredith assured herself as she left the office, she had more important things to worry about.

Kathleen had been quite desperate in her attempts to send a message earlier.

The most likely place to meet with the ghost seemed to be the flower beds, and that's where she intended to go. If there was the slightest chance she could see Kathleen again she might be able to understand what it was her late friend was so frantic to tell her.

She turned the corner of the corridor and almost collided with the two figures approaching from the opposite direction. At first she merely glanced at the two women, but then she took a closer look and uttered a shocked gasp. "Great good heavens, whatever happened to you both?"

Olivia and Grace stood close to each other, their chins drooped and their eyes downcast. Olivia held a bucket while Grace clung to a kitchen chair. Both women looked as if they'd been caught in a torrential downpour.

Water dripped from their hair and from the end of their noses. Their saturated clothes clung to their bodies and small puddles began forming around their feet.

Grace was the first to speak. "We had an accident, m'm," she mumbled.

"Yeah," Olivia said. "We tipped a bucket of water all over us."

Meredith stared in amazement. "How in heaven's name did you manage to do that?"

The young women glanced at each other and lapsed into guilty silence.

If Meredith hadn't been quite so taken up with the problem of Kathleen's ghost, she would have demanded a full explanation. As it was, she was in far too much of a hurry to waste time just then. "Never mind," she said, waving her hand in the direction of the kitchen. "Go at once and get those wet clothes dried out. I'll speak to you about this later."

"Yes, m'm." The two women scurried past her, and as Meredith continued on her way she heard one of them mutter, "See? I *told* you we'd end up in the workhouse."

Shaking her head, Meredith walked out into the cool, damp air. Summer, it seemed, was on the wane, and soon the autumn winds would bring the leaves fluttering down from the trees.

She hoped that Kathleen's dilemma could be resolved before winter set in. The thought of the poor woman drifting about the school grounds in the bitter cold was most distressing. That was, she amended, if ghosts could indeed feel hot or cold.

As she crossed the wet grass, she spotted Tom trimming the rosebushes in front of the assembly hall windows. Hurrying across the lawn toward him, she reminded herself to ask him about the memorial gardens.

He looked up as she approached, and straightened as much as his stooped shoulders would allow.

"I went to see Davie's mother this morning," she said, when she reached him. "Apparently Davie has a stomach ailment, but Mrs. Gray assured me he'll be back to work tomorrow."

Tom grunted. "He needs to be, m'm. I've got a lot of work on me hands. Can't do it all by meself. These old bones aren't what they used to be."

Feeling guilty, Meredith cleared her throat. "Yes, well, I'm afraid I have a little more work for you. We've decided to make a memorial garden for Miss Duncan, to commemorate her work. We'd like you to dig a flower bed. Nothing elaborate, of course, just a small plot where we can plant annuals every year and hold a service."

Tom's watery eyes regarded her with disbelief. "A garden, m'm?"

"Just a small flower bed, Tom." Meredith glanced in the direction of Kathleen's flower beds. The sun shone bright on the blossoms without a hint of mist anywhere. "Just like those." She pointed at the flowers. "Only smaller, of course. The students will be planting the flowers. All we need from you is to dig the bed. Somewhere under the trees, perhaps?"

"Dig the bed," Tom repeated, in the same tone of utter disbelief.

"Yes, Tom." Meredith looked at him, hoping he wouldn't flatly refuse. "Perhaps Davie could help you."

Tom looked at her a moment longer, then bent back to his rosebush. "Davie can dig it," he said, snapping the pruning shears at a tendril.

"Er . . . good." Meredith hesitated, then asked, "Ah . . . when do you think it will be finished?"

"Just as soon as Davie gets to it."

And she would have to be satisfied with that, Meredith thought.

She left him, eager now to get to the flower beds and see Kathleen again. It was strange that her late friend had chosen to appear only to her, and seemingly no one else. How much simpler the problem would be if Felicity and Essie could see the ghost, too.

True, they had agreed to help her hunt down Kathleen's killer, but all the time they suspected her of hallucinating she was at a distinct disadvantage when it came to passing on whatever clues Kathleen's ghost might provide.

Arriving at the flower beds, she was pleased to see that Tom had finished the weeding, and the soil had been raked smooth between the blossoming plants.

Apparently Kathleen had been appeased as well, since she failed to materialize, though Meredith waited until the very last minute before reluctantly returning to the school for the midday meal.

At least for now, she thought with rueful resignation, she would have to rely on her own instincts. Whatever Kathleen had been trying to convey would have to wait.

Chapter 12

The rest of the day passed uneventfully, and when Felicity and Essie joined her for a quiet evening in the library, Meredith was happy to sit and relax in her favorite brocade armchair.

"Will Sylvia be joining us?" Essie asked, as she sank onto one end of the davenport.

"I believe she had some tasks she wanted to attend to in her room."

Meredith frowned as Felicity muttered, "Thank the Lord for small mercies."

Somehow she would have to try to settle the differences between Felicity and Sylvia. Not now, though. This was a time to relax and enjoy the quiet of the evening.

The moment they were settled, however, Felicity leaned forward and in a low, conspiratorial whisper asked, "So tell us, Meredith, did you talk to that little hussy, Deirdre Lamont?"

"I did, indeed." Meredith recounted her conversation

with Deirdre. "I do believe she intends to keep her word," she added, as Felicity nodded in satisfaction. "She seemed quite concerned when I mentioned speaking to her parents."

"I can imagine." Felicity leaned back and stretched out her feet in front of her. She still wore her high-buttoned boots, and wriggled her toes as if trying to ease a cramp. "I've met Deirdre's father. Lord something or other. Never can remember his name. Anyway, he's quite formidable and short of temper. I imagine Deirdre would do just about anything to avoid bearing the brunt of his anger."

"Well, I hope she has enough sense not to meet up with Mr. Silkwood again."

"He's not even pleasant to look at," Essie murmured. "I can't imagine why a young girl like Deirdre would be the least bit interested in a man like that."

Felicity sniffed. "Some people will do anything for attention." She turned to Meredith. "Anyway, what's going on with your ghost? Has it popped up with any more clues?"

In spite of Felicity's rather dry tone, Meredith decided to take the question at face value. "As a matter of fact, I saw Kathleen in the classroom this morning."

Essie gasped, covering her mouth with her slender hand, while Felicity's eyes gleamed with anticipation.

"That must have been interesting." She leaned forward, propping herself up with her hand on her knees. "Do tell. What did she have to say? Did the girls get a glimpse of her? I hope she was wearing something more becoming than that misty shroud thing you described."

Meredith raised her chin. "I absolutely refuse to discuss the matter any further until you can take me seriously."

Felicity leaned back again, her expression remorseful.

"Oh, very well. I promise to listen and not make fun of you. Or Kathleen, rest her soul."

Meredith gave her a suspicious glance, then said cautiously, "She kept pointing at the pupils. She seemed agitated about something."

"She was always agitated with the pupils. They probably weren't paying enough attention to you."

Meredith shook her head. "She keeps trying to tell me something and I'm fairly certain it has something to do with her murder, but I can't understand what it is she's trying to say."

"It's a shame you can't simply ask her what she wants." Felicity shook her head. "If you ask me, Meredith, if you really want to find out who killed Kathleen you have to stop relying on her ghost and tackle this problem another way."

Essie nodded. "I have to agree, Meredith dear. You do seem to be going around and around in circles with all this ghost business."

Meredith looked at them both in exasperation. "What do you suggest I do?"

"Tackle this thing the way P.C. Shipham would. That's if he had half a brain." Felicity sighed. "What I'm saying is that we should be following the clues that we have and trying to discover what they mean."

"That's just the problem." Meredith rose to her feet. "We don't have any real clues to go on. All we have is a noncommunicative ghost, unreliable at best, who appears only to me in an extremely unstable form and who seems obsessed by her flower beds."

Felicity nodded. "Put like that, the solution does seem somewhat remote. Perhaps we should be actively searching for clues?"

"In what way?"

Essie jumped to her feet, waving her hands. "I know! What if we search the clothes Kathleen was wearing that night?"

"They've been sent on to her relatives." Meredith lifted her hands and let them fall. "I really don't know what to do next. I know poor Kathleen will not rest until her killer has been brought to justice. I just wish she could give me a better clue than flowers."

Felicity smothered a yawn and pushed herself up from her chair. "Well, I don't know about you but I'm ready for bed. Let's discuss this in the morning, when we're all a little more clearheaded."

Meredith followed her two friends into the corridor, wondering if she would ever be clearheaded again.

Alone in her room, she undressed in a hurry, anxious to get under the cozy eiderdown on her bed. For some reason the air seemed to have cooled considerably.

Pulling the sheet up under her chin, she turned on her side and closed her eyes. Seconds later she snapped them open again as the back of her neck started to tingle in a most disturbing way.

She saw immediately the cause of her discomfort. Blinking her eyes, she stared at the faint greenish glow hovering in the corner of the room.

"Kathleen," she whispered. "Is that you?"

The glow moved from side to side.

Reaching out a hand, Meredith snapped on the light.

The green glow turned white, faded, and reappeared, then swirled into a misty cloud. Very slowly, in the middle of the cloud, Kathleen's face appeared. Her two arms appeared to be separated from her body, and floating of their own accord.

Alarmed, Meredith realized that either she was losing

her ability to see the ghost, or Kathleen's power to materialize was fading. Either way, it presented an urgency to solve the murder before time ran out and she could no longer communicate with her dear, departed friend.

"Tell me," she said quickly. "Any way you can. Tell me who did this to you. I want to help, but I'm still in the dark. You have to help me."

For a moment it seemed the apparition would fade away, then for a brief moment Kathleen's face peered out at her with sightless eyes. One arm lifted and a fluttering finger pointed across the room.

Meredith turned her head and stared at the still life hanging on the wall. Hardly surprising, the oil painting depicted a cottage garden crammed with blossoming shrubs and flowers.

She turned back to the ghost. "I know it has something to do with flowers, but you'll have to give me more. . . ." She let her voice trail off when she realized she was talking to a blank wall. Once more, Kathleen had disappeared.

Meredith stared at the vacant spot in dismay. What if Kathleen couldn't come back to her? What if her killer were never caught? Would Kathleen then be trapped in a sort of netherworld—doomed to wander forever without any hope of concluding her journey?

A tear slid down Meredith's cheek. She couldn't bear the thought of it. Somehow she had to find the killer, and give her friend the peace she so richly deserved.

Snuggling under the covers again she sent up a fervent prayer. It didn't feel quite right, praying for a ghost, but when one became desperate one snatched at any port in a storm. And right then, Meredith desperately needed a safe harbor.

She awoke to the sound of the rising bell, surprised at how well she had slept. Having quite expected a restless night, she felt refreshed and more alert than she had of late.

After dressing in a black skirt and pearl pink waist, she hurried down to the dining hall, determined to be first at the breakfast table.

As it was, she had barely seated herself when the chattering girls poured into the room. After returning the greetings of the pupils seating themselves at her table, she studied their expectant faces.

Saturday was the one day the students were allowed to go into the village unescorted, on the understanding they would remain together in groups of three or four. Not all of them took advantage of the opportunity, but those who did had to receive permission,

Meredith was not entirely comfortable with the arrangement, but since it had been tradition at Bellehaven for several years before she became headmistress, she felt obligated to honor it, as long as it didn't cause any undue problems for the rest of the school.

"Now," she said, giving each girl a stern glance, "who would like permission to visit the village this afternoon?"

Several girls held up their hands. Amelia and Loretta both wanted to go, as did Penelope, who had apparently recovered from her grandmother's death enough to enjoy an outing.

Meredith gave her permission, then shut out the conversation at the table to wrestle with her own problems.

It was all very well for Felicity to say they should hunt down clues, but where to start? There didn't seem to be any logical place to look. Perhaps that dratted constable had been right when he'd said it was a vagrant who had

now disappeared. Then again, if that were so, then why did
Kathleen keep pointing at flowers?

Deep in her reverie, she paid little attention to the girls
slipping away from the table. The dining hall emptied out,
and still she sat there, alone and deeply anxious over the
fate of her late friend.

Her tea had cooled, and she reached for the cup, irritated at herself for spoiling her favorite part of breakfast. If
there was one thing she couldn't stand, it was cold tea.

Absorbed in her frustration and concern, she failed to
notice the gentleman enter the hall until he stood in front
of her.

"Ah! Mrs. Llewellyn. There you are!"

His deep voice, seemingly coming out of nowhere, startled her so much she hastily dropped the cup on the saucer
and slopped some of the tea over the side.

Looking up, she smiled sheepishly into the penetrating
eyes of Stuart Hamilton.

"I trust Miss Montrose is fulfilling her duties as expected?"

Meredith blinked. Unsettled by Hamilton's commanding gaze, she had trouble remembering who Miss Montrose was, let alone if she was fulfilling any duties.

He raised one languid eyebrow. "Is something wrong?"

Flustered, Meredith cleared her throat. "Not at all, Mr.
Hamilton. I was simply phrasing my answer before ex-
pressing it to you."

Stuart Hamilton laid his hat on the table. Flipping the
tails of his coat, much to Meredith's discomfort, he sat down
next to her. "It is that difficult to enlighten me?"

"Oh, good heaven's no." In a near panic, she sought for
something sensible to say. "Miss Montrose is doing an excellent job, as far as I can tell. After all, she has yet to com-

plete a full week here. Any judgment on my part would surely be somewhat premature, wouldn't you say?"

Amusement gleamed in his dark eyes. "I have the utmost faith in your judgment, Mrs. Llewellyn. I'm under the impression that you are an excellent judge of character and quite capable of using your talent instantaneously."

"Really." She eyed him warily. "Well, I thank you for your confidence, Mr. Hamilton. I sincerely hope you will not be proven wrong in the case of Miss Montrose."

He held her gaze much too long for comfort. She looked down at her hands, surprised to see them gripping each other as if expecting never to see one another again.

"Somehow I sense that all is not well with your new instructress. I'd be obliged if you'd advise me of any potential problem."

She made herself smile at him, though she couldn't quite meet his discerning gaze. "Not at all. It is nothing more than the settling in of a new tutor. It takes time, but I'm quite sure Miss Montrose will be a commendable addition to the staff of Bellehaven."

"Admirably put." Hamilton leaned back in his chair and stuck a thumb in his waistcoat pocket.

Meredith found the gesture mildly disturbing, though she couldn't have explained why. His next words, however, deepened her distraction.

"Then perhaps you'll tell me what *is* concerning you enough to mar such a pleasant face with a frown."

"I . . . it's just . . . well, I don't really . . ." She let her voice trail off, at a loss how to explain.

Hamilton leaned forward, his face creased in concern. "Something *is* troubling you, Mrs. Llewellyn. I must insist you tell me what it is."

In the end she just blurted out the words. "I believe

that someone here in Bellehaven is responsible for Miss Duncan's unfortunate demise."

He straightened, his brows raised in shock. "On what do you base this disturbing theory?"

Again she floundered. She could hardly tell him that she'd been visited by Kathleen's ghost. He'd have her committed to a lunatic asylum. Which could well be where she belonged, she thought, with a cold touch of fear.

Sitting there with him in the empty dining hall, the idea that Kathleen could come back from the dead to haunt her and goad her into a full-scale investigation of her death seemed ludicrous.

Yet she only had to think back to the night before, with the ghost hovering at her bedside, one finger shakily pointing at a painting, to renew her convictions.

She raised her head. "You said you trusted my judgment. I hope it is enough to accept the fact that I am convinced someone in this school cruelly hit Miss Duncan in the head with that tree branch and killed her. Since I do not have the cooperation of the constabulary, I am doing my best to discover who that person is myself."

Stuart Hamilton stared at her for a long moment, then slowly rose to his feet. "I suggest, Mrs. Llewellyn, that you concentrate on the matters at hand concerning the pupils of Bellehaven, and leave police work to those far better suited for it."

Why did she imagine he would give her the benefit of the doubt? Meredith wondered. Even her two close friends had trouble believing in her theories. How could she expect a man like Stuart Hamilton to accept the ramblings of a woman with whom he had little acquaintance?

She got up from her chair, pausing to allow him to draw

it back for her. "Thank you, Mr. Hamilton. I shall do my best to follow your advice."

His expression was full of suspicion, but he gave her a brief nod, reached for his hat, then turned briskly on his heel and strode across the floor to the door.

Long after his footsteps had faded away, Meredith stood scowling after him. Infuriating man. Pleasant face, indeed. Rather impudent of him.

Even so, her mouth twitched into a smile at the memory.

In the next instance she gave herself a stern mental shake. She had work to do and not a moment to spare.

She found Essie and Felicity in the music room, discussing a tune that Essie hesitantly picked out with one finger on the piano.

"It has something to do with a bicycle," Felicity declared. "A tandem, unless I'm much mistaken."

"No, no." Essie shook her head. "It's the name of someone. I'm sure of it."

Meredith shook her head and crossed the room. "It's 'Daisy Bell.' Written by Harry Dacre about twelve years ago." She sat down at the piano and deftly played the entire song, singing the words as best she could with her somewhat inadequate voice.

"Bravo!" Essie clapped her hands as Meredith finished the tune with a flourish of chords. "A wonderful performance."

"Indeed," Felicity agreed. "Though I do question how you became so familiar with a bawdy music hall song."

Meredith smiled as she rose from the piano. "That's for me to know and you to wonder."

Felicity's expression suggested she was not about to let the matter rest there.

Meredith, however, had a more important subject on her mind. Looking around to ensure they were quite alone, she added quietly, "I saw Kathleen again last night."

Essie gasped, while Felicity merely looked skeptical. "Where was she this time? Tucked up in your bed?"

Meredith gave her a sour look. "As a matter of fact, she was in my room. She kept pointing a finger at my Harold Peto painting."

Essie whispered, "The one with all the flowers in front of the cottage?"

"Exactly. Flowers again." Meredith shook her head. "For some reason, Kathleen keeps pointing at flowers, but I can't for the very life of me imagine what they could possibly have to do with her death."

"Maybe she's not pointing at the flowers." Felicity gently closed the lid of the piano. "She could have been pointing at the cottage."

So utterly delighted was Meredith that at long last Felicity was accepting the fact that there actually was a ghost with whom she could communicate, marginally at least, the significance of her friend's words escaped her at first.

"Why would Kathleen point at a cottage?" Essie sat down on the stool and folded her hands in her lap. "There's no cottage on the school grounds. Not unless you count the gardener's cottage."

Meredith stared at her. "Oh, my goodness. Why didn't I think of that?"

Felicity laughed. "I hope you're not suggesting Tom went after Kathleen with a tree branch. As I keep telling you, it's more likely to be his assistant. Perhaps that's what Kathleen has been trying to tell you."

Meredith shook her head. "I talked to Davie's mother.

She is absolutely certain Davie was in the house all evening on the night Kathleen was killed. He's not the one."

"Just when did you talk to Davie's mother?"

Felicity had an edge to her voice, and Meredith said hurriedly, "Yesterday morning. I forgot to mention it last night."

Felicity grunted. "I don't know how you expect us to help you if you don't tell us everything."

"I'm sorry." Meredith laid a hand on her arm. "I'm afraid so much was happening yesterday, it quite slipped my mind. I won't forget again."

Felicity nodded. "Good. Then let's all go down to your room and study that painting. There may be something else there that can help us understand what that dratted ghost is trying to tell you."

Chapter 13

Standing in front of the painting a few minutes later, all three tutors studied it in silence.

"I can't see anything except the cottage, flowers, and the sky," Essie announced. She glanced nervously over her shoulder. "Kathleen isn't here right now, is she?"

"Not as far as I can see," Meredith assured her. She peered closer at the painting. "These aren't even the same flowers that Kathleen planted in the flower beds. Look at those Canterbury bells. They are enormous."

Felicity grunted. "I can't see why everyone makes so much fuss over this Peto person. Not my cup of tea. Look at those tiny butterflies. Quite out of proportion in my opinion."

Meredith gazed fondly at her prized possession. "That's exactly why I love his work. Everything is so detailed. Look at the colors in those wings. Why, I—" She broke off as something occurred to her.

Both women stared at her—Felicity with resigned expectation and Essie with sheer panic.

"What is it?" she cried, one slender hand at her throat. "What do you see? Is it Kathleen? Where is she?" She looked wildly around as she backed toward the door.

Felicity rolled her eyes at the ceiling, while Meredith held out her hand to the terrified woman. "It's all right, Essie. I can't see Kathleen so I'm quite sure she's not here."

"So what *did* you see?" Felicity demanded with barely controlled impatience.

"I've just remembered something." Meredith sank onto the edge of her narrow bed. "When I talked to Deirdre yesterday I noticed she wore a butterfly brooch."

"Oh, she's always wearing that thing," Felicity muttered. "I'd wager a month's salary that disgusting Silkwood gave it to her. I don't think . . ." Her voice trailed off, while she exchanged a significant look with Meredith.

"Deirdre," Meredith said softly.

Felicity shook her head. "I might have said she'd do just about anything to keep Kathleen from talking to her parents, but murder? That seems a little excessive, don't you think? I can't say I'm fond of the girl, but she doesn't strike me as a cold-blooded killer."

Essie whimpered, earning another scathing scowl from Felicity.

"Anyone is capable of murder, given a strong enough motive." Meredith pushed herself up from the bed and walked to the door. "Even one of us."

Felicity smiled, while Essie burst into hot denials.

"Oh, no, no, no! Not me! I couldn't. I simply couldn't kill anyone!"

"Yes," Meredith said firmly. "You could. When cornered,

we women are capable of anything. Our instinct for survival is every bit as strong as any man's." With that, she opened the door.

Essie rushed out, obviously upset. Felicity followed more slowly, turning to Meredith as she closed the door.

"I take it you'll talk to Deirdre again?"

"Most certainly." Meredith met her gaze. "I'll relate every word to you, I promise."

"Very well." Felicity glanced down the corridor, but Essie had already disappeared. "I don't know what we should do about Essie. I fear she doesn't have the stomach for this kind of activity."

"You may be right." Meredith started down the corridor. "But she would be devastated if we didn't include her. You know how sensitive she is about being left out of things."

"She is terribly insecure." Felicity's long stride took her past Meredith, and she paused in order to allow her friend to catch up. "She must not have had a satisfying childhood." She glanced at Meredith out of the corner of her eye. "Does she ever talk about it? Her home life before Bellehaven, I mean. She appears to come from a very good family. I have to wonder how she came to be teaching in a finishing school, instead of attending one."

Meredith hesitated. It was not her place to tell Felicity Essie's story. On the other hand, if it would help Felicity understand the young woman and arouse her sympathy, she might not be so belittling toward her.

In the end, propriety won, and she kept silent on the subject. If Essie wanted Felicity to know her background, then it was up to Essie to enlighten her. Until then, Meredith assured herself, she would keep the young lady's secret.

Parting company with Felicity, she headed for the

library—the most likely place to find the students if they had chosen not to go into the village.

Crossing the entrance hall, she was just in time to see Tom disappearing out the door. She hurried after him, certain he must have been looking for her.

He was halfway down the steps when she stepped outside and called out his name. He paused, taking his time to turn around and face her.

"I was going to come back later, m'm."

"That's all right, Tom." She started toward him. "Do you have something to tell me?"

"Yes, m'm. Davie's back. Seems a little better. In his spirits, I mean. Doesn't say much about what's bothering his stomach."

"Oh, good. I am glad."

"He's digging the flower bed for you, m'm. Just like you asked." He turned and pointed to the center of the woods. "In that little clearing in the woods. Thought you'd like it there. Nice and private, it is."

Touched by his thoughtfulness, she smiled at him. "Thank you, Tom. That would be perfect. Please let me know when it's finished. Oh, and could you fetch some annuals for the students? Marigolds would be nice. Five dozen should be plenty. I know it's late in the season, but you should get them for a good price now, shouldn't you?"

Tom nodded and touched the brim of his panama. "Don't you worry, m'm. I'll see to it."

She watched him hobble down the stairs, pleased that the plan was coming together. It was ironic, she thought, as she retraced her steps, that Sylvia, a near stranger, should be responsible for the idea. Then again, Sylvia was now a part of Bellehaven, a member of the family, so to speak. Felicity would just have to get used to that.

Much to her delight, she saw Deirdre the minute she entered the quiet library. The girl sat in a corner, her nose buried in a book. She looked up as Meredith approached, her eyes wary and her expression hard as stone.

"I'd like you to come with me to my office," Meredith said softly, so the other girls lounging around the room couldn't hear.

A flash of defiance crossed Deirdre's face. Then she shrugged, laid down her book, and followed Meredith in silence all the way to the office.

Once inside the darkly paneled room, Meredith closed the door and indicated a chair with a wave of her hand.

Deirdre slumped down on it and stretched her feet out in front of her.

"That is no way for a lady to sit," Meredith said sharply. "Straighten your back, cross your ankles, and tuck them under your knees, the way you've been taught."

Deirdre's scowl darkened as she obeyed the command.

"That's better." Meredith edged behind her desk and sat down. "Now, I have something to ask you and I must warn you to be perfectly honest with me. I shan't be able to help you unless you tell me everything, and mark my words, the constable will not be nearly as understanding as I will be."

Deirdre's defiance vanished in a look of stark terror. "The constable? What does he have to do with me? I haven't done anything."

"Well, that we shall see. Now answer me carefully. Do you know anything about what happened to Miss Duncan on the night she was killed?"

Deirdre's look of surprise seemed quite genuine. "Miss Duncan? No, miss, I don't. All I know is she went out walking and someone hit her on the head."

Meredith continued to look into the girl's eyes. She saw confusion, then a dawning sense of shock.

Deirdre leapt to her feet. "You think I did it? You think I hit Miss Duncan? But I didn't! I wouldn't! I wasn't even there."

"Then perhaps you can tell me exactly where you were that evening."

"I was in the music room, rehearsing for the Harvest Festival concert." Tears sprang to Deirdre's eyes. "There were six of us there. Ask any of them." She waved a hand at the door "They'll tell you I was there."

Meredith raised a hand to silence the girl's outburst. "It's quite all right, Deirdre. I believe you. Now please sit down."

She sat, sniffling and hunting for a handkerchief.

Meredith watched her for a moment, then added quietly, "I trust you are no longer seeing Mr. Silkwood?"

Deirdre gave a violent shake of her head. "No, miss. He wouldn't see me again, anyway. He was really angry and upset with me when I told him that Miss Duncan had threatened to tell my parents about us. He said he'd deny everything, and that I was lying. He forbid me to ever go near him again."

Meredith struggled to control her anger. Men like Silkwood should be hung, drawn, and quartered. "I would say you are well rid of someone who treats you like that."

More tears slid down Deirdre's cheeks. "I only went to meet him because he was kind to me. He gave me things and said I was pretty. He was much nicer to me than my own father."

And there it was, Meredith thought, with a wave of compassion. The poor child was looking for a substitute to

replace her callous father. When would men ever learn to
embrace their children, instead of governing them?

"Well, you have learned a hard lesson. I hope you remember it well."

"Yes, Mrs. Llewellyn." Deirdre sniffed again.

"And for heaven's sake, blow your nose."

She blew, long and hard, into the wisp of white cotton.
"Thank you, Mrs. Llewellyn," she murmured, when she'd
tucked the handkerchief back into her sleeve.

"You are now dismissed."

Obediently, Deirdre got up from her chair and slipped
from the room.

Meredith absently rearranged the pens in the tray holding her inkwell. So Victor Silkwood had been extremely
upset to learn that Kathleen intended to notify Deirdre's
parents about their association. Upset enough to silence
Kathleen permanently, perhaps? No doubt he would not
want his wife to know about his indiscretions, particularly
with a young lady of such a tender age.

Frowning, she glanced at the clock. The trick was to
find out where he was and what he was doing the night
Kathleen died. This seemed an auspicious time to pay the
Silkwoods a social visit.

Meredith broached the subject after the midday meal
as she left the dining hall with Felicity and Essie. "I've
decided to pay Victor Silkwood a visit," she announced,
as the three of them strolled down the corridor to the
lounge. "We need to sell more tickets to our Harvest Festival concert, and the Silkwoods would be a good place to
start."

Felicity stared at her. "The Silkwoods? Have you completely lost your mind? Didn't you just tell me that he was
behaving like a cad with Deirdre Lamont? Why would you

invite such a despicable creature to attend a concert with our young ladies?"

Meredith sighed. "Under the circumstances, I think it is extremely doubtful that he would actually attend the concert. I merely want to use the sale of the tickets as an excuse to get some information."

"What kind of information?"

"Such as where that gentleman might have spent last Saturday evening."

Felicity paused at the door to the lounge, her eyebrows raised in comprehension. "You are suggesting that Victor Silkwood killed Kathleen?"

Essie, who had been trailing behind them as usual, reached them just as Felicity uttered the incredulous words.

"Oh my goodness!" Essie slapped a hand over her mouth. "Mr. Silkwood is a murderer?"

Fortunately her words were muffled by her hand.

"Shush!" Meredith looked quickly over her shoulder, then opened the door to the lounge and ushered her friends inside. After making quite sure they were alone, she said quickly, "We are only speculating at this point. Which is why we need to go to the Silkwood mansion."

"Now?" Essie looked as if she were about to step off a high cliff.

Felicity clicked her tongue. "Perhaps it would be better to leave Essie here. After all, if we are to trick that scoundrel into admitting he killed Kathleen, we can't afford to let him know our purpose."

Essie lowered her hand. "I want to be part of this. I want to come with you."

Meredith smiled at her. "Of course you shall come, Essie. We are going to need your assistance."

Essie's eyes widened. "In what way?"

"I've always maintained that if one wishes to know something, the best source is the servants. Therefore, while we are talking to Mr. and Mrs. Silkwood, we will need someone to slip away and charm the Silkwood's butler into answering a question or two."

Felicity uttered an skeptical laugh. "And you expect Essie to do the charming?"

"Who else?" Meredith laid her hand on Essie's arm. "You have to admit, Felicity, that a man would be hard-pressed to ignore the appeal of this face."

Felicity pursed her lips. "No doubt, but is she up to it? You know how she goes to pieces at the slightest provocation. What if she gives away our real purpose for the visit?"

"I do wish you would not speak of me as if I were not here." Essie raised her chin at Meredith. "I will be happy to talk to the butler and you can rest assured, he will not know the reason for me asking questions."

"Good. Then let us go now." Meredith opened the door again. "Felicity, if you would be so good as to fetch the tickets for me? I will go to the kitchen and ask Mrs. Wilkins to make up a basket for Mrs. Silkwood. A few of those delicious macaroons should enhance our welcome, don't you think?"

"Without a doubt." Felicity grinned. "I had no idea you were so devious."

"One does what one has to do," Meredith murmured. "Essie, ask Reggie to get the carriage ready for us. Tell him we shall need him to drive us to the manor."

Essie nodded, then sped away, her skirts fluttering around her ankles as she disappeared around the corner.

"You're really going to trust her with such an important task?" Felicity's face registered doubt. "Essie can be so scatterbrained at times."

"She has a natural ability to charm money out of a miser." Meredith closed the door of the lounge. "I'm quite sure she'll be able to worm what we need to know out of any man. He would be utterly unable to resist."

Felicity snorted. "Well, it's a good job you're not asking me to do the charming. I'd as soon wring a man's neck to get what I want out of him."

"Which is precisely why we need Essie." Meredith patted her arm. "Do fetch the tickets for me. I'll meet you at the carriage in a few minutes."

Muttering something unintelligible, Felicity strode off down the corridor, almost colliding with a group of girls coming the other way.

Meredith headed in the opposite direction to the kitchen, where she found Olivia on her knees in front of the oven, stoking the coals with Mrs. Wilkins standing over her.

Quickly Meredith explained what she wanted, and the cook wasted no time in packing up a dozen or so coconut macaroons and a few maid of honor cakes to go along with them.

Felicity and Essie waited impatiently by the carriage when Meredith hurried out into the sunny outdoors. Of Reggie there was no sign.

"He said he had to mend a window lock," Essie explained. "He promised he wouldn't be long."

"We might as well wait in the carriage then." Meredith opened the door and scrambled up inside.

Felicity gave Essie a little push and she climbed up, too. The carriage bounced and rocked as Felicity took her seat opposite them.

"I do love the smell of leather," Essie said, patting the seat. "It's such a comforting smell."

"Stinks of wet horses if you ask me." Felicity peered out

the window. "How long is that dratted man going to—"
She broke off with a sharp exclamation.

"What is it?" Meredith leaned forward to peer out the
same window. "What did you see?"

"Miss Montrose. She's over there talking to Reggie. I
hope he's not telling her where he's taking us."

Meredith frowned at the two people on the other side of
the courtyard. They had their heads together in a suspi-
ciously conspiratorial manner. "I didn't know she was ac-
quainted with Reggie," she murmured.

Felicity sat back with a look of triumph. "I knew there
was something peculiar about that woman."

"She's most likely asking him about a repair," Essie
pointed out. "After all, he is responsible for the maintenance of the building."

"Well, I shall ask him when he gets over here." Felicity
scowled at the window. "If he ever gets over here."

She was still frowning when Reggie approached the carriage and opened the door. "Good afternoon, ladies!" He
grinned at them all. "All ready for our little jaunt to the
Silkwoods' manor, are we?"

"We've been sitting here twiddling our thumbs for at
least ten minutes." Felicity glared at him. "What was so
important you kept us all waiting like fools while you talked
to that dratted woman?"

Reggie looked surprised. "Miss Montrose? She wanted
to know if there was a place in the village where she could
buy nails."

"Nails?" Meredith stared at him, as did her two companions. "What on earth would Miss Montrose want with
nails?"

Reggie shrugged. "Beats me. I told her as how I had
nails she could have, but she said she wanted a lot of them

and preferred to buy them herself. I sent her down to Wilfred, the ironmonger. He's got plenty of nails in his shop."

"Did she happen to ask for hammers, too?" Felicity wanted to know.

"No, she didn't." Reggie frowned up at the clear blue sky. "Wonder why she didn't."

"We don't have time to worry about that now," Meredith said sharply. "Make haste, Reggie. I'm quite anxious to be on our way."

"Yes, m'm. Right away, m'm." Reggie touched the brim of his cap with his fingers, then climbed up onto his seat. Gathering up the reins, he clicked his tongue, and Major slowly pulled forward, his powerful shoulders straining to take the weight of the carriage.

Inside, Felicity settled back against her seat. "Well, I hope the Silkwoods are at home after all this."

"It might be as well if they are not." Meredith turned her head to gaze out of the window. "It would give us a better opportunity. . . ." In that instant she quite forgot what she'd started to say.

They were passing the flower beds, and she could see quite clearly the white cloud with Kathleen floating in the middle. She seemed agitated, shaking her head in such a vigorous manner Meredith wondered for a moment if it would fly off her transparent body.

A tremor of apprehension shook Meredith's body. Was Kathleen trying to warn her? Was she leading her friends into danger at the Silkwoods' mansion?

Chapter 14

"Meredith? Whatever's wrong with you? You look as white as a . . ."

Felicity's voice trailed off and Essie uttered a soft shriek. "Ghost! You were going to say ghost, weren't you." She stared wide-eyed at Meredith. "Did you see Kathleen again? Did you?"

Meredith leaned back. "Just a trick of the light, I'm sure." She smiled at Essie. "Are you ready to talk to the Silkwoods' butler? Have you rehearsed what you will say to him? You will need to be careful how you phrase your questions."

Seemingly reassured, Essie shook her head. "I'm sure it will come to me. I have no trouble talking to men." She slid a glance at Felicity from under her eyelashes. "Unlike some people."

Felicity sniffed. "When you know as much as I do about men, you won't want anything to do with them, either."

"I know more than you think." Essie smoothed her

gloves more securely over her fingers. "Enough to know that the right words and gestures can get you almost anything."

"Nothing but trouble in my experience." Felicity's face was grim as she stared out the window. "Nothing but terrible trouble."

Essie was immediately contrite. She leaned forward, and laid a hand on Felicity's knee. "I'm sorry. I didn't mean to upset you."

Felicity shook her head. "You didn't." She shifted her knees away from Essie's hand. "I'm quite sure you will get the answers we need."

"I hope so," Meredith murmured. "I would dearly love to get this matter settled once and for all, then perhaps we can all find peace with Kathleen's death." Including Kathleen, she added inwardly.

"It wouldn't surprise me at all to find out Victor Silkwood killed her. He is such a despicable creature." Felicity shuddered. "Heaven preserve us all from such monsters. They should be banished from the earth."

"We shouldn't jump to conclusions," Meredith reminded her. "Though I do think we should be on guard while we are there. A desperate man will stop at nothing to hide his sins."

"Don't I know it." Felicity glanced at Essie. "You will be careful?"

"I shall be extremely careful," Essie assured her.

The carriage jerked to a halt, surprising them all. "We are here already?" Meredith stared through the window. "Goodness, that didn't take as long as I thought." She didn't want to admit as much to the others, but now that they were actually at the steps of the Silkwood mansion, butterflies were battling each other inside her stomach.

Perhaps she had been a trifle hasty in insisting that they visit a suspected murderer. What if something dreadful happened to them? She would never forgive herself for leading her two friends into danger.

She was on the verge of telling Reggie to turn about and return to the security of Bellehaven, but Felicity had already jumped out of the carriage and was marching up the steps. Chills chased down Meredith's spine as she saw her friend grasp the bell pull and give it a firm tug.

Essie ducked her head and stepped down to the ground, then turned to look at Meredith. There was nothing left to do except climb down after her.

Reaching the ground, she looked up at Reggie, who had rather belatedly arrived to give the ladies a hand. "Wait here for us," she told him. "If we seem to be taking an inordinately long time, please do feel free to inquire after us."

Reggie looked surprised at this unusual request, but gave her a quick nod. "Very well, m'm. How long do you think I should wait?"

"When Major starts getting restless should be a good time." Feeling only a little less apprehensive, Meredith started up the steps to join her friends.

The door was opened, as she expected, by the butler—a tall, well-proportioned man with graying hair and keen dark eyes. Much to her satisfaction, she saw his gaze linger on Essie a fraction longer than necessary. It seemed the young woman would have no trouble engaging the man in conversation.

Handing the butler her calling card, Meredith announced, "I and my fellow tutors wish to speak with Mr. and Mrs. Silkwood, if it's convenient."

The butler glanced at the card, then ushered them into

the spacious foyer and asked them to wait. As he disappeared down a narrow hallway alongside the impressive sweep of staircase, Essie whispered, "He's rather imposing, don't you think?"

"Bosh," Felicity said rudely. "The way the man looked at you it's obvious he'll fall under your spell the minute you flutter those ridiculously long eyelashes of yours."

Essie had the grace to blush. "I hadn't noticed," she murmured.

Meredith's heart was thumping so uncomfortably she hardly took in what they were saying. She watched with anxious eyes for the butler's return, and when he reappeared, she had to clear her throat to speak. "I do hope we are not intruding at an inconvenient time?"

The butler bowed his head. "Not at all, madam. Mr. Silkwood will be happy to receive you in the drawing room. This way."

He crossed the foyer and grasped the handles of two very tall doors. Pushing them open, he walked inside the room and stood back to allow them to enter.

Meredith led the way, her fascination chasing away her fears. The room glowed with color. Purple velvet curtains hung at the lofty windows, and several paintings, splashed with vivid hues, hung on the pale lilac walls.

The cream satin chairs and peach ottoman added a pleasant contrast to the colorful Persian rug spread in front of the marble fireplace, and a large aspidistra spread its leafy arms across one corner of the room.

The butler waited until they had seated themselves, then, with a slight bow, he withdrew, leaving them to gaze around in silence.

Felicity was the first to speak. "A little gaudy, don't you think?"

"I like it," Essie declared. "It's quite bright and cheerful."

"So is a circus ring," Felicity muttered, "but I wouldn't want to live in it."

Meredith was saved from answering by the return of the butler. Standing just inside the door, he announced, "May I present Mr. Victor Silkwood."

He stood back and a portly gentleman entered, wearing a brilliant peacock blue waistcoat under his dark jacket. He wore a monocle in one eye, and his red nose bore testimony to his fondness for spirits. "Good afternoon, ladies."

All three tutors chorused a greeting.

"My wife offers her apologies," he said gruffly. "Unfortunately, she is indisposed at present."

"I do trust it's not a serious ailment? Perhaps this basket of fine delicacies from our cook will help improve her constitution." Meredith met the cold gaze with a little shiver. She was quite sure that Mrs. Silkwood had not been informed that the tutors from Bellehaven were present in her home.

Victor Silkwood could only guess at the reason for their visit, and no doubt suspected that his dallying with Deirdre Lamont was the cause. He would not want his wife to hear what he would undoubtedly deny, should they bring up the subject.

Meredith longed to tell him what she thought of his behavior, and indeed was afraid that Felicity would do just that, judging by that lady's furious expression. She hurried to forestall her friend before she could blurt out an accusation that would surely land them in hot water.

"We shan't keep you long, Mr. Silkwood. Our business here today concerns the annual Harvest Festival concert held at Bellehaven."

Silkwood's expression would have been comical had it not been for the seriousness of the situation. His eyes

widened, allowing the monocle to drop from his eye and
swing lazily at the end of its chain bouncing against his
protruding stomach.

He snatched it with one hand, and at that moment Essie
rose to her feet.

"Pardon me," she said, her voice trembling. "I find myself in a great need to use the powder room, if I may?"

Silkwood eyed her with far too much familiarity, in
Meredith's opinion. She dare not look at Felicity to see her
expression.

"Of course," Silkwood said, his thick lips curving in an
ingratiating smile. He reached for a velvet pull rope and
gave it a sharp tug. "Summersby will escort you, my dear."

"Will you manage alone, Miss Pickard, or would you
like me to accompany you?" Meredith asked, giving Essie
what she hoped was a meaningful look.

Essie gave a slight shake of her head. "I can manage,"
she said bravely. "Thank you, Mrs. Llewellyn."

The door opened once more, and Summersby filled the
doorway.

"Please escort this young lady to the powder room,"
Silkwood said, devouring Essie with his eyes. "See that she
returns safely."

Summersby bowed his head, then took a step back and
waited for Essie to pass by him before closing the door behind him with a gentle click.

Meredith found that she had been holding her breath,
and she let it out on a soft sigh as Silkwood advanced
deeper into the room.

"Now," he said, fitting his monocle back in his eye.
"What's all this about the Harvest Festival?"

"We were wondering if you and Mrs. Silkwood would
care to attend the concert." Meredith opened her pink silk

handbag and took out the tickets. Holding them up, she murmured, "The price is very reasonable."

Silkwood stared at her for a long moment, while the silence in the room thickened. Meredith became aware of the loud ticking of a clock on the mantelpiece. Out of the corner of her eye she saw Felicity plucking at her skirt—a sure sign she was agitated.

"And is that the real reason for your visit?" Silkwood asked bluntly.

Startled, Meredith dropped the tickets. She bent down to retrieve them from the floor, her mind desperately searching for a suitable response. She could hardly accuse the man of murder with nothing but her own suspicions for evidence.

As for his liaison with Deirdre, that had been dealt with, and much as she longed to do so, a reprimand at this point would only cause more trouble for everyone, particularly if the loathsome man was innocent of Kathleen's demise.

Nevertheless, he obviously expected her to answer him, and the longer she hesitated, the more suspicious he would become. Taking a deep breath, she straightened and looked him in the eye.

Staring into Silkwood's icy gaze, she made an effort to speak calmly. "Why yes, Mr. Silkwood. We are trying to sell as many tickets as possible to raise funds for the school."

It wasn't exactly a lie, she consoled herself. Although tickets were usually reserved for families of the pupils, now and then a few were sold to the villagers if there were enough left over.

Silkwood continued to stare at her in a manner that made her most uncomfortable. She looked at Felicity for help, but her friend sat stone-faced, her eyes fixed on the door as if willing it to open.

Meredith looked back at Silkwood. "We'll quite understand if you'd rather not attend."

His face darkened, and she wondered uneasily what she'd said to further upset him. At that moment, however, the door burst open and Essie rushed in.

"Do please excuse me," she said breathlessly, coming to an abrupt halt. "I was so afraid you'd leave without me." She looked at Meredith and wiggled her eyebrows up and down in an urgent signal that announced to one and all she had significant news to impart.

Victor Silkwood apparently had interpreted the message. He stared hard at Essie, his lips pressed together in an ominous thin line.

Felicity jumped to her feet, saying briskly, "Well, we won't waste any more of your time, Mr. Silkwood. We're sorry to have inconvenienced you." She inclined her head at Meredith. "We must get back to Bellehaven now."

Meredith rose. "Do give our kind regards to Mrs. Silkwood. I trust she will be feeling better soon." She started forward, flicking her fingers at Essie to indicate she should leave at once.

She had barely reached the door, with Felicity hot on her heels, when Silkwood's harsh command cut across the room. "Just one moment."

Meredith halted, so suddenly Felicity barged into her, sending them both into Essie who appeared to have frozen to the spot. She uttered a squeak of surprise as the three of them smacked into the door.

For a moment Meredith had trouble getting her breath. Untangling herself from the other two, she straightened her hat and turned to face Victor Silkwood.

He stood looking at her with an odd expression on his face. If she hadn't known better, she could have sworn he was amused about something. With a sly, half smile he took a few slow steps toward her, his hand outstretched.

She shrunk back, bumping once more into Felicity, who immediately stepped around her and stood bravely in front of her. She opened her mouth to speak, and Meredith cringed at the prospect of what her friend might say.

Before she could utter a word, however, Silkwood said smoothly, "I'll take two of those tickets. Summersby will pay you for them on your way out."

Felicity snapped her mouth shut, while Meredith went limp with relief. Handing the tickets over, she murmured, "We are much obliged to you, Mr. Silkwood. I hope you enjoy the concert."

She didn't wait for his response. Turning swiftly, she gently shoved Essie out the door and followed close behind her. The door slammed to as Felicity joined them.

"Whew," she said, mopping her brow with the back of her hand. "I thought that repulsive ogre was about to attack us. I was quite prepared to—" She broke off abruptly as Summersby appeared from out of the shadows.

"If you would wait here a moment, ladies." He inclined his head, then opened the door of the drawing room and disappeared inside.

Afer a moment or two, during which Meredith wondered uneasily if they were indeed out of danger, he reappeared.

"I've been instructed to make payment to you for concert tickets," he announced, addressing Meredith."If you wouldn't mind waiting a few more moments while I fetch the money."

Meredith was sorely tempted to tell him the tickets were a gift, but that would only raise more suspicions as to the reasons for their visit, so she merely nodded.

Summersby glided away down the corridor and out of sight.

"Mr. Silkwood couldn't have killed Kathleen," Essie whispered.

Meredith exchanged a skeptical glance with Felicity. Leaning closer to Essie, she whispered, "How can you be sure of that?"

"Because he was here last Saturday night. He spent the day shooting grouse and held a shooting party that evening. He never left the house."

Felicity stared at her in disbelief. "How did you get that man to tell you all that?"

Essie's lips curved in a smile. "It wasn't that difficult," she said modestly.

"Never mind that." Meredith sighed. "Now we are no further along in our investigation. We still don't know who killed Kathleen, and the longer it takes to find out, the less chance we have of ever apprehending the murderer."

"Especially if it turns out the killer was the vagrant after all," Felicity murmured.

"No," Meredith answered her sharply. "I refuse to believe that. I am convinced the killer is connected to Bellehaven. Kathleen has made that very clear."

"Or at least as clear as a ghost can."

Meredith was about to answer when Summersby emerged from the shadows once more. She opened her palm to receive the coins he held in his fingers and he dropped them into her hand. "Thank you," she murmured.

In silence he led them to the door, though Meredith

noticed he gave Essie a smile as she passed by him and stepped out onto the terrace. The door closed behind them, and they descended the steps.

Reggie met them at the bottom. "I was just coming to see if you were all right," he said, shoving some kind of reading material into his back pocket. "Major has just started shuffling about."

It was a good job they hadn't been in any danger, Meredith reflected, as she climbed up into the carriage. If they'd relied on Reggie to save them, they could all be lying dead by now.

She settled back on the seat with mixed feelings. It was a relief of sorts to learn that Silkwood couldn't have killed Kathleen. If he hadn't had an alibi, she wasn't sure what her course of action would have been.

P.C. Shipham would have been difficult to convince, and most reluctant, no doubt, to investigate such a prominent member of the community without incriminating evidence.

The problem with this crime-solving venture was that she had no evidence whatsoever to work with, except for her unpredictable connection to the departed victim. Not exactly satisfactory when chasing down a murderer.

Not that she was an expert on such matters, but having read of criminal investigations in the newspaper, it seemed that the constables had an abundance of clues to follow, whereas she was forced to wait around for the nebulous indications of an erratic ghost. No wonder she was floundering in the dark.

Felicity's sharp voice jolted her out of her musing. "For heaven's sake, Meredith, take that scowl from your face. If the wind changes, your face will look like that forever."

Essie giggled. "My mother always told me that as a

child. It worried me, and every time I went out in the wind I would try to keep a smile on my face so that if the wind changed I'd at least have a pleasant face to look at."

Felicity studied her for a moment then said dryly, "If only I'd known."

Essie frowned, obviously at a loss, and Meredith hurried to intervene. "Well, at least it wasn't entirely a wasted visit. We sold two tickets to the concert."

"Don't be too surprised if they don't attend," Felicity said as she examined her high-buttoned boots. "I can't imagine that man would risk bringing his wife to a place where she is likely to run into his paramour. I would even go so far as to suggest that Miss Lamont is not the only object of his lust."

Essie uttered a shocked gasp. "I certainly hope you are mistaken, Felicity. Our young ladies are at the age where they are easily led astray." She glanced at Meredith. "That can lead to all sorts of trouble."

Felicity eyed her curiously. "You sound as if you are expert on the subject."

Essie raised her chin. "Maybe I am."

Felicity leaned forward. "Come, Essie, tell us what you know."

A dull flush crept across Essie's cheeks. "I prefer not to talk about such things."

"We are here," Meredith announced loudly, relieved for the opportunity to interrupt the conversation. Felicity could be most persistent when her curiosity was aroused. Essie's past was her own business, hers to divulge as she saw fit to whomever she chose.

Upon entering the school, she was delighted to find the entrance hall ablaze with color. Tom had kept his word and boxes of plants covered the floor next to the stairs.

"We'll call a special assembly before supper," Meredith announced, as she followed Felicity and Essie up the stairs. "We can hold the memorial service right after church tomorrow."

"Doesn't give us a lot of time," Felicity muttered. "Who's going to give the speech?"

"I will. I'll work on it tonight. The sooner we do this the better. I just wish we'd thought of it earlier."

"Well, I'm sure Kathleen won't mind the wait."

Meredith gave her a sharp look, but Felicity seemed perfectly sincere, and she had to give her friend the benefit of the doubt.

Besides, she had other things on her mind. She had a speech to write, and a ghost to appease. For surely Kathleen would hear her words, and that made the task all the more formidable.

Chapter 15

The following morning, having completed the speech to her satisfaction, Meredith was eager to get to church. It was where she had first seen Kathleen's ghost, and she was hoping to have another chance to communicate with her late friend.

Her last glimpse of the ghost's fiercely shaking head had stayed with her, and she itched to know the reason for it. If it was a warning, it must not have anything to do with Victor Silkwood, since he was elsewhere the night she died.

Seated inside the vast walls of the church, Meredith peered time and time again at the empty pew in front of her. She barely heard a word of the sermon, and felt the reverend's eyes on her more than once. No doubt she was in for another meaningful comment about her lack of attention when she left. In spite of her vigilance, however, Kathleen's ghost failed to appear.

As instructed, the students changed clothes as soon as

they returned to Bellehaven after the church service, and eventually assembled around the freshly dug flower bed in the woods.

Each of them carried a plant plucked from the boxes in the foyer. Meredith had worked hard on her speech, and delivered it with pride. She spoke of Kathleen's achievements, and those of some of her pupils. She related anecdotes of her friend's life at the school, and mentioned Kathleen's devotion to her duties, her love for her students, and her pride in being such an integral part of Bellehaven.

"Kathleen Duncan will be missed by one and all," she finished, "and we dedicate this flower garden in her memory. May the plants in it grow and flourish, like the students under her masterful wing."

Polite applause accompanied her as she stepped over to the flower bed and knelt in the dirt. Taking up the trowel Tom had provided, she planted the bright yellow clump of marigolds, then stood up. "Thank you, Kathleen," she murmured.

She half expected to see the cloud form over the little flower bed. After all, surely Kathleen would be tempted to attend her own memorial service.

But the air remained clear and sunny as the students knelt one by one to plant their offering and say a small prayer. As the last few girls approached, Meredith caught sight of Stuart Hamilton standing some distance away among the trees.

While she was still wondering if he'd been there all the time, he slowly stepped back out of sight and did not return.

Once more the midday meal was a subdued affair, and when it was over, Meredith decided to pay one more visit to the main flower beds, just in case Kathleen should decide to come back there.

Casting a critical eye over the plants, she noticed the blossoms looked rather dejected—hanging their heads under the late summer sun. Meredith wondered if Tom had been watering them as much now that Kathleen wasn't there to keep him on his toes. She stooped down to take a closer look at the bedraggled chrysanthemums. Normally they would flourish right through October, at least.

Shaking her head, Meredith lifted a crimson head on one of the plants. The color seemed faded, the petals limp. Cold with dismay, she let the head fall. Kathleen would be devastated to see them like this. She would have a word with Tom right away and see that he watered the flower beds.

She stepped back, allowing her gaze to roam over all the beds, taking in the new weeds. It never failed to amaze her how fast plants dried out, while weeds seemed to flourish no matter how little moisture they acquired. More evidence of Tom's neglect.

Clicking her tongue in annoyance, she leaned over and grasped the lower stems of a clump of dandelions and gave them a hefty tug. Pleased to see the root had emerged intact, she stepped back. At the same time a wisp of smoke floated across the flower beds and came to rest several feet away.

No matter how many times she saw it, she still felt unnerved by the sight of Kathleen's face peering out at her from that eerie cloud of mist. "I'm glad you're here," she said, trying to ignore the awkwardness of addressing an apparition. "I hope you saw the ceremony at your memorial garden. We wanted to commemorate your hard work and dedication, and keep your memory alive."

The ghost swayed back and forth, but gave no indication of understanding.

Meredith tried again. "I'm sorry, Kathleen, but I'm afraid I have no idea how to go about finding out who killed you. I've tried, but either there just aren't enough clues to help me, or I'm not clever enough to ferret out the truth."

A languid, translucent hand rose in the air and one long finger pointed to the flower beds.

"Yes, I know," Meredith said, a trifle impatiently. "The killer has something to do with flowers. The problem is, I don't know how the two things connect. Every possible suspect has been eliminated."

Kathleen's head shook from side to side and the finger slowly moved in Meredith's direction and stayed there.

"Me? I'm a suspect?" Meredith stared at the ghost in disbelief. "You can't honestly think for one moment that I would hit you on the head with a tree branch?"

Again the head shook, but the finger remained pointed at Meredith.

Feeling totally at a loss, she took a step closer. "Kathleen, I understand that you are unable to cross over into the spiritual world until your killer is found and punished. I wish there was something I could do to help, but really, I have done all I can."

The ghostly finger swung toward the flower beds and back to Meredith.

Frustrated, Meredith raised both her hands. "I wish you could show me something I could understand!"

The finger rose with the movement of her hand, and fell again.

Meredith stared at her fingers, which still clutched the clump of dandelions. "Tom did the weeding," she protested. "This was simply one he missed."

The finger remained steadily pointed at the dandelions.

Frowning, Meredith stared at the yellow petals. Was it something about the color? "I don't understand—"

She turned as a shout interrupted her. Felicity's long stride brought her swiftly to Meredith's side. "I've been looking for you everywhere," she said, the second she was within earshot. "You'll never guess what that silly nincompoop has done now."

Glancing back at the flower beds, Meredith was not really surprised to see that Kathleen's ghost had vanished. With a sigh of resignation, she turned back to Felicity. "Which nincompoop is that?" she asked mildly.

"Why, that Montrose woman, of course. Why are you picking dandelions? Is this some new form of floral arrangement?"

Meredith looked at the weed in her hand. "I've just pulled it from the flower bed. Tom must have missed it when he weeded them."

"Tom misses a lot of things. Good job he has Davie to help him. Goodness knows what he'd do if Davie ever decided to leave."

"We would have to look for a new assistant for Tom, that's all."

"We certainly would. That old man can barely hobble around, much less do hard work like weeding flower beds."

Meredith didn't answer. She was thinking about the ghostly finger persistently pointing at the dandelions. Perhaps Kathleen hadn't been pointing at flowers all this time after all. Maybe she'd been pointing at weeds.

How could she have forgotten the first time she'd seen Kathleen up close, and the first time she'd spoken to her? *Don't worry, Kathleen. I'll make sure Tom gets the beds weeded.*

Her ghost had made it clear from the first.

Not that it helped matters much, of course. She was no closer to finding a connection to weeds than she had been to flowers.

But at that moment the words clicked in her mind, bringing back a sharp memory of Amelia's outburst in the classroom. She had been far more emotional over Kathleen's death than anyone else, and yet just a day or two earlier, she'd been severely chastised by the teacher. For mistaking weeds for flowers.

Good heavens. Was it possible the humiliation had been enough to send Amelia chasing after Kathleen with a tree branch? But she couldn't have. She was in her room all evening with Loretta Davenport. Loretta herself had confirmed that.

"Goodness, Meredith, you are in a bit of a funk today. What's bothering you? Not worrying about that dratted ghost again, are you?"

Meredith shook off her muddled thoughts and smiled at her friend. "You haven't told me what Sylvia Montrose has done to upset you so."

"Nails," Felicity said, puffing a little as she stomped across the grass. "She's stuck nails all over the wall of Kathleen's classroom. The place is peppered with the pesky things."

"What on earth for?"

"She's nailing all sorts of things to the walls. Instructions for the girls, dinner party menus, list of household supplies, duties of servants, things like that."

Meredith frowned. "Why doesn't she write them on the blackboard?"

"I asked her that." Felicity shortened her stride as they reached the edge of the lawn. "She said she prefers permanent reminders of her lectures, so the girls don't forget what they've learned. She believes that seeing the lists on the walls every day will help them memorize them."

"But all that hammering!"

"She doesn't use hammers." Felicity stuck her hands into the pockets of her skirt as she stalked across the courtyard. "She's got some newfangled nails that she can just push into the wall. She showed me one. It looks like a nail except it's got a large round head that she pushes with her thumb. Calls it a drawing pin, or something like that."

"How odd. I shall have to take a look at it."

"Yes, well, a hole's a hole, that's what I say. No wonder Kathleen's ghost keeps popping up all over the place. She's probably turning in her grave at the thought of that blasted woman puncturing her classroom walls."

"It's no longer Kathleen's classroom," Meredith gently reminded her. "It belongs to Sylvia now, to do with as she sees fit. As long as she doesn't do any serious damage, I really can't see the harm."

Felicity muttered something under her breath, but once again Meredith wasn't listening. She had just caught sight of Amelia and Loretta huddled together inside one of the tennis courts, and judging by the way they were waving their arms about they were engaged in a serious argument.

She watched them for a moment or two, then decided it might be a good idea to intervene. "I'll join you and Essie for supper," she told Felicity, and without waiting for an answer, sped across the grass to the tennis courts.

Meredith was not normally one to eavesdrop on someone's conversation, but as she drew nearer to the two young ladies it occurred to her that she might learn something helpful if she didn't reveal her presence.

Slowing her pace, she skirted the lawn and crept behind the trees until she was level with the tennis courts. Moving as close as she could get without being seen, she peered around the trunk of a sturdy beech tree.

The girls were still there but were no longer arguing. At least, their voices were no longer raised. Amelia was facing in her direction, saying something to Loretta, but her voice was too low to carry through the trees.

Meredith squinted hard, grateful for her excellent vision as she stared at Amelia's lips. She couldn't quite catch all she said, but it seemed as if Amelia was threatening Loretta to keep quiet about something. Then, quite distinctly, Meredith deciphered the young woman's next words.

"I'll tell Mrs. Llewellyn you're sneaking out to see your boyfriend every night."

Meredith drew back, her mind racing to her conversation with Deirdre Lamont. *I'm not the only one sneaking out to meet a secret boyfriend.*

If Loretta was in the habit of leaving the school to meet someone, it was also quite possible that she'd lied about being in her room the night Kathleen was killed. If that were so, that would leave Amelia without an alibi. There was only one way to find out. She must talk to the girl at once.

"It's feeling chilly in here." Grace rubbed her arms and shivered. She walked over to the oven and touched it with her fingertips. "No wonder! The stove is cold." She swung around to look at Olivia, who stood at the sink peeling potatoes for supper. "Did you forget to put more coals in it?"

Olivia dropped the knife with a splash into the water. "Oh, crikey! I'll do it now." She rushed over to the stove and bent low to look inside the furnace. "It looks like it went out. I'll have to light it again. Fetch me the morning newspaper while I get the sticks."

"What if Wilkie hasn't read it yet?"

"Too bad. Mona'll be here any minute to do her Sunday inspection, and if I don't have this stove lit she'll have another excuse to dock me days off. Mrs. Wilkins will have to do without her Sunday read, that's all."

"She'll be cross with you." Knowing there was no use arguing with her friend, Grace walked over to the pantry to get the newspaper. Olivia rushed by her to get the dry sticks that would set the coals on fire.

"Oh, no!" At Olivia's shriek, Grace flew out of the pantry, the newspaper in her hand. "Now what?"

"There aren't any sticks in here." Olivia pointed to the large wooden box at her feet. "It's empty."

"Oh, yeah. I used the last of them to light the stove this morning." Grace thrust the newspaper at her. "Here, you crumple this up and I'll go get some more sticks."

"Why on earth didn't you get them this morning?" Olivia demanded, furiously crumpling up sheets of the newspaper.

"I didn't have time, did I." Grace rushed to the door and hauled it open. "I won't be a minute. They're right there in the shed."

"Get a move on then." Olivia glanced at the clock on the ledge above the stove. "For gawd's sake hurry up. Mona'll be here any second."

"I'm going, I'm going." Feeling just a little put upon, Grace fled to the shed. After all, if Olivia had remembered to add more coals to the fire, she wouldn't be looking for sticks to light it again.

Inside the musty shed she saw a pile of the slim pieces of wood. Reggie must have chopped them that morning. Olivia wouldn't like that. The sticks would be damp and hard to light. Quickly she gathered up a pile and rushed back to the kitchen, dropping one or two as she went.

Olivia knelt in front of the stove, shoving wads of paper into the furnace. "Quick, give me the sticks." She held out her hands and Grace dropped the pile into them.

Some of them scattered all over the floor, and Olivia glared at her. "Pick them up and put them in the blinking box. I won't need all these."

"Stop giving me orders," Grace muttered, with a rare show of defiance. "Who put you in charge?"

"Just hurry up." Olivia thrust the sticks in on top of the paper. "If Mona catches us doing this, we'll both be in bad trouble."

"It's all your fault." Grace bent over to pick up the wood. "And you're supposed to crisscross the sticks or they won't catch fire."

"Who says." Olivia took the matchbox out of her apron pocket and slid the drawer open. "I can light them any way I want."

"Suit yourself." Grace carried the sticks over to the box and dropped them inside. When she turned around again Olivia was leaning close to the furnace, her cheeks puffed out as she blew on the burning paper. She kept puffing and puffing, her face growing redder by the minute.

"I told you they wouldn't light like that," Grace said, feeling superior for once.

"It's because they're damp, silly." Olivia scowled at her. "If you'd remembered to fill the box this morning they'd be dry by now."

"And if you'd remembered to add the coals—"

"Oh, shut up." Turning back to the stove, Olivia leaned closer into the furnace, pulled in a deep breath, and blew her lungs out.

The paper flared up and yellow flames leapt between the sticks. Olivia shrieked and drew back, flames eating at the bib of her apron.

"Take it off!" Grace screamed, rushing to help Olivia tear off the burning apron.

Olivia balled it up and threw it at the sink. It landed on the back edge, and both girls sagged in relief.

"You could have been burned to death," Grace said, close to tears as she hugged her friend. "It's all my fault. I'm sorry I forgot the sticks."

"No, it was my fault for forgetting the stupid coals." Olivia sounded shaken, and her cheeks were drained of color. "I shouldn't have leaned in that close. Look, it's scorched me dress. I just hope it didn't burn me bodice. It's the only good one I've got." She pulled out the neck of her dress to peer down inside it.

"Well, the fire's lit again now." Grace pointed at the stove. "Better close the door and let it draw."

"Let's hope it gets warm by the time Mona gets here." Olivia moved closer to the stove and slammed the door shut. "Look at this mess on the floor. Sawdust everywhere. Help me clean it up before Moaning Minnie sees it."

"I'll get the mop, you get the dustpan and brush." Grace headed for the pantry again. "Good job Mrs. Wilkins went up to talk to Monica. Let's hope she keeps her talking up there a bit longer."

She reached into the corner for the mop, while Olivia bent over to pick up the dustpan and brush from the ledge under the shelf. Straightening, she wrinkled her nose. "It smells awfully smokey in here, don't it. Perhaps we should open the back door for a bit to let it air out."

"Mona will wonder why it's open," Grace said, walking

back into the kitchen. "Then we'll have to—" Her words were cut off by her shriek as she dropped the mop.

Olivia walked out behind her. "Now what?" She gasped. "Oh, my gawd."

Grace could hardly believe her eyes. The kitchen curtains on both sides of the window were ablaze, the flames creeping rapidly up to the ceiling.

Olivia rushed over to the sink and started slopping water out of it with her hands. Potatoes and peel flew everywhere as she yelled, "Get me a blinking basin!"

Heart thumping in fear, Grace jerked open a cupboard just as the door opened and Mrs. Wilkins walked in.

"I'm quite sure you'll find the kitchen spick-and-span as usual," she said, then stopped dead, her gaze glued to the flaming curtains.

Monica appeared in the doorway, her mouth dropping open with shock. For a moment everyone just stood there, staring, then Mrs. Wilkins rushed into action.

She grabbed the basin from Grace's shaking hands and shouted, "Go at once and ring the alarm bell. Tell the teachers there is a fire and get the girls outside. Olivia, find Reggie and send him here immediately."

Grace didn't wait to see what happened next. She bolted past Monica, who still seemed incapable of movement, and flew out the door, followed by Olivia. As they bounded up the steps, she prayed, "Please, Lord, don't let the school burn down. Oh, *please*, don't let it burn down!"

Chapter 16

Meredith started forward, intending to confront the young women on the tennis courts. She had barely taken a couple of steps when the strident sound of the school bell echoed across the lawns.

She halted, staring across the grass at the gray walls of the building, trying to imagine why the bell would be ringing in the late afternoon. It couldn't possibly be time for supper yet.

Then, as she started walking slowly toward it, she saw a steady stream of pupils spilling down the front steps. Praying that it was merely a safety drill and not anything more serious, she sped toward the school.

As she rushed up the steps, she was forced to fight her way past the girls scrambling down them. Essie stood in the doorway, her white face pinched with fright. Her voice trembled as she urged the pupils to hurry.

"What's happened?" Meredith demanded, puffing to catch her breath.

"There's a fire in the kitchen." Essie grabbed her arm. "Mrs. Wilkins is down there with Monica. They told us to evacuate but—"

"Where's Felicity and Sylvia?" Meredith peered down the hallway, but could see no sign of either tutor.

"They're going around the rooms to make sure everyone is out." Essie wrung her hands. "Oh, I do hope they won't get trapped up there."

"Has anyone sent for the fire brigade?"

Hearing a commotion behind her, Meredith swung around. Three of the pupils had tried to get out the door at the same time and were fighting to get ahead of each other.

"Ladies!" Meredith grabbed a flailing arm and dragged the girls apart. "One at a time. Please. Remember what you've been taught. Decorum at all times. Even in times of grave danger. We must . . ." She broke off, aware of how utterly ridiculous that sounded.

In any case, she was talking to thin air. The girls had fled through the door and out of sight.

"I don't know if anyone sent for the fire brigade," Essie said, peering down the corridor. "Do you think all the students are out now?"

"I'm sure Felicity will make sure they are all safe." Meredith patted her arm. "I'd better find out about the fire brigade. Why don't you go outside and make sure the girls don't panic and run away or something."

Essie nodded, close to tears. "What if the school burns down? What will happen to us?"

"We're not going to lose the school," Meredith said firmly. "Now cheer up, Essie. Stiff upper lip. Set an example for the pupils."

Essie nodded, and she left her, hoping and praying that her conviction held up. Bellehaven was home to her—to all of them, Felicity, Essie, Mrs. Wilkins, Monica . . . even Sylvia now, she supposed. What would they all do if the school burned to the ground?

Determined not to dwell on that, she headed for the stairs and ran down them. She could now smell the smoke. A cold chill of apprehension robbed her of breath as she reached the kitchen. Dreading what she might see, she threw the door open.

Mrs. Wilkins and Monica stood in front of the sink, scooping water out of it in basins and throwing it at the window. Charred remains of the curtains hung dismally from the rails, still smoldering, with wisps of smoke curling up to the blackened ceiling.

A quick glance around assured Meredith that the fire was contained to the window area and she hurried forward to give the women a hand.

"We should get those down and dump them in the sink," she said, gesturing at the tattered curtains. Reaching out, she grabbed the back of a kitchen chair and pulled it forward.

"Be careful, Mrs. Llewellyn," Monica warned. "It's bound to be hot up there. You could get a nasty burn."

"I'll be careful." Meredith climbed up on the chair and steadied herself before reaching for the railings. Carefully she touched the end of the rod. It felt warm, but not too hot to handle.

She unhooked the rod, slid off the ornamental end, and then tilted the rod so that the curtain rings rattled down it and allowed the smoldering material to fall into the sink.

A faint spitting sound could be heard as the curtains hit the cold water. "I'll open the window," Meredith said, leaning forward to reach the handle. "We need to get the smoke out of here."

It dismayed her to see the scorched frames. They would all have to be repainted. Thank heavens the glass didn't break with the heat.

Grunting with exertion, she pushed down the handles and opened both the windows, then started to climb down from the chair.

"The curtains are good and soaked now," Mrs. Wilkins said, relief making her voice sound high. "Thank the Lord the fire didn't get into the ceiling or we would have had a nasty problem, that's for sure."

"The smoke certainly has made a mess of the ceiling," Monica remarked, nudging her nose skyward.

Meredith looked up, one foot on the ground, to view the damage. At that moment, a wall of cold water hit her with such a force it knocked her off the chair.

Stunned, she could only lie on the floor for several seconds while water poured over the sink, cascading down on her head and shoulders.

Vaguely she heard Mrs. Wilkins screaming Reggie's name, over and over. Spluttering and shaking, Meredith fought her way to a sitting position and the downpour mercifully stopped.

"Oh, my, oh, my." Water dribbling from her flattened hair, Monica kept muttering the words over and over as she held out her hand and helped Meredith to her feet.

More water formed a puddle from Mrs. Wilkins's saturated skirt as she shrieked at Reggie through the window. "We got the fire out, you blithering idiot! Who told you to use the hose in here, for pity's sake?"

Stroking wet hair out of her eyes, Meredith peered through the soggy window at Reggie.

He stood holding the dripping hose in his hand, a sheepish look on his face. "Sorry, ladies!" he called out. "Olivia told me the window was on fire so I brought the hose. Didn't mean to soak you."

Meredith opened her mouth to speak, but just then a deep voice roared out from behind her.

"What in blazes is going on here?"

She swung around to see Stuart Hamilton transfixed in the doorway, his face frozen in shock.

Miserably aware of how she must look, shirt soaked and clinging to her, strands of wet hair dripping rivulets of water down her face, Meredith nevertheless tried to make the best of things.

"Good afternoon, Mr. Hamilton. We were just having a small setback. Nothing serious." In an effort to appear unaffected, she patted her wet hair in place as best she could. "Everything is under control."

Hamilton's gaze roamed over the drenched kitchen floor, the blackened window frame and smokey ceiling, then back to the three bedraggled women. "So it appears."

"Oh, Mr. Hamilton, sir," Monica said, her wheedling voice sounding quite unlike her usual harsh tones. "The maids somehow set fire to the curtains. We managed to get it out without too much damage."

"I'm surprised you arrived here so quickly," Meredith observed, determined to take his mind off the disfigured window frame.

He switched his gaze to her face, and she stared back, determined not to be intimidated by his obvious disapproval. "I happened to be passing by the school gates," he said gruffly, "when I heard the bell ringing. I saw students pouring down the steps and came to investigate."

"Ah." She nodded, fixing a fragile smile on her face.

"Well, no harm done, as you can see, save for a slight soaking. If you will excuse us, we must see that our pupils return to their rooms before we change into dry clothes."

His gaze shifted down her body to her feet and up again. Her hands curled into tight fists at her sides. Arrogant beast! How dare he!

"In my unworthy opinion," he said lazily, "you might all do well to get into dry clothes immediately. Before you all catch your death of cold. I'll see that the students return to their quarters." With that, he turned on his heel and left, letting the door swing to behind him.

"Oh, Lord," Mrs. Wilkins murmured. "That was most unfortunate."

"It certainly was." Monica sneezed, and hunted for a handkerchief in her pocket. She dragged it out, soaking wet, and tried ineffectively to wipe her nose. "Not a very good indication of how this establishment is run." She glared at Meredith as if the entire catastrophe were all her fault.

"I'll see the maids are severely punished," Mrs. Wilkins said, giving Meredith a worried look.

"There's no need for that." Meredith picked up her wet skirts and headed for the door. "I'm sure it was an accident. I will have a word with them myself later, once we have restored order."

She winced as she opened the door. The clanging bell still echoed down the corridor. "I suggest you both change your attire before you do anything else."

"I'll go and tell Grace to stop ringing that blinking bell," Mrs. Wilkins muttered as she followed Meredith into the corridor. "You won't get into trouble with Mr. Hamilton over this, will you, m'm?"

Meredith smiled at her and raised her voice to be heard above the bell. "Please don't worry about that, Mrs.

Wilkins. I can deal with Stuart Hamilton. He may try to intimidate everyone with his roaring lion performance, but I assure you, underneath that arrogant breast lies the heart of a gentle lamb."

In the shadowed stairwell she failed to see the figure at the top of the stairs until a movement caught her eye. She looked up, once more into the cool gaze of Stuart Hamilton. And there was absolutely no doubt in her mind that he'd heard every word she'd said.

It seemed an eternity until Hamilton spoke. When he did, his voice sounded deceptively calm. "That's considerably flattering, Mrs. Llewellyn. I should remind you, however, that I hold you responsible for the smooth operation of this institution and would have no hesitation in voicing my displeasure if things were not as they should be. I trust that I can depend on you to see that doesn't happen?"

"Without question, Mr. Hamilton." Feeling like an utter fool, she marched up the stairs toward him.

The foyer bustled with activity as students swarmed through on their way to their rooms. Meredith caught sight of Felicity herding a large group of chattering girls up the stairs.

She turned at that moment and met Meredith's gaze. Her eyes widened in shock, and her mouth dropped open as if she were gasping for air.

If Meredith needed confirmation of how awful she must look, Felicity's reaction told the tale. Lifting her chin, she turned back to Hamilton. "If you will excuse me," she said, pitching the words above the babble all around her, "I have business to attend to right away."

He bowed, but not before she'd seen that infuriating flash of amusement in his eyes. "Oh, by all means, Mrs. Llewellyn. Please don't let me detain you."

"You can rest assured, Mr. Hamilton, I shall allow you to do no such thing." With that, she swept past him and as elegantly as her sodden clothes allowed, headed for the stairs.

It wasn't until that evening that Meredith had a chance to question Loretta. Alerted to the fact that the young lady had a habit of slipping out to meet her boyfriend, immediately after supper Meredith stationed herself at the end of the corridor where she had a clear view of the room that Loretta shared with Amelia.

She didn't have to wait too long before the door opened and Loretta's head appeared around it.

Drawing back, Meredith waited until the young woman drew level with her before stepping out of the shadows. "Loretta, may I have a word with you?"

Loretta froze, her face growing pink. "Mrs. Llewellyn! I was just going outside for a breath of fresh air. All that smoke in the school this afternoon has affected my lungs and I fear I shall not be able to sleep if I don't clear them."

"Oh, I won't keep you long." Meredith walked with her to the stairs. "I want to talk to you about the night Miss Duncan died."

Loretta threw a frightened glance at her. "But I told you I don't remember her saying anything about where she was going that night."

Meredith paused at the top of the stairs. "I have an idea you don't remember because you didn't see Miss Duncan that night. Am I right?"

Again Loretta gave her one of those scared looks. "Yes, miss. I mean no, miss. I was there when she brought Amelia the book."

"I would really think twice before lying about this,

Loretta." Meredith pinned a stern gaze on the frightened girl's face. "You were meeting a friend of yours that night, were you not? It has come to my attention that it's a frequent occurrence for you."

Loretta stumbled back and sank against the wall. "I'm sorry, miss. I know it was wrong, but he can only get away at night and I'm not allowed out at night by myself—"

"For good reason," Meredith said, shamelessly interrupting her. "It is for your own protection."

"Yes, miss." Loretta hung her head.

"So you lied about being with Amelia that night?"

"Yes, miss." Loretta raised her chin. "She always lies for me when I go out and I didn't want to get her in trouble because of me."

"I see." Meredith hesitated, then added quietly, "Do you know if Amelia went out that night?"

Startled, Loretta shook her head. "No, miss, I don't. Amelia doesn't go out much. Not like some of the girls. I don't think she went anywhere that night."

"Did she seem . . . different when you came back?"

The girl seemed confused, no doubt wondering why she wasn't being scolded for disobeying the rules. "Different? In what way, miss?"

"Nervous? Upset about something?"

Loretta stared at her for several long seconds, then burst out, "Surely you're not thinking it was Amelia who killed Miss Duncan?"

Meredith sighed. "We don't know who killed Miss Duncan, Loretta. I'm simply trying to find some answers to that question, that's all."

"Well, it wasn't Amelia. It couldn't have been. No, Mrs. Llewellyn, you're wrong. Amelia wouldn't hurt anyone. I know she was upset about being scolded in class, and she felt everyone was laughing at her and that made her a little bitter, but she would never, never *kill* someone."

Meredith nodded. "Very well, Loretta. I must ask you not to tell Amelia about our conversation. There's no point in upsetting her further."

"No, miss. I won't say anything to her at all."

"Good." Meredith started to turn away, then paused. "Oh, and Loretta? No more sneaking out to meet boyfriends. If I find out you've broken the rules one more time, you'll be sent home in disgrace. Do I make myself clear?"

"Yes, Mrs. Llewellyn." Loretta turned and trudged gloomily down the hall back to her room.

Meredith waited until the door had closed firmly behind the young woman before returning to her own room. Sinking onto the edge of the bed, she went over her conversation with Loretta.

Apparently Amelia had been protecting her friend's secret all this time, lying whenever it was necessary to cover for her. She could also have been lying about her own whereabouts the night Kathleen had died. There just seemed no way to prove that one way or another.

Meredith gazed around the room. "Kathleen? Are you there?" She waited, hoping to see the familiar white cloud form. Perhaps over there, by the sturdy wardrobe that housed her dresses. Or by the dresser, where her silver-backed brush and comb gleamed in the flickering glow from the gas lamp nearby.

Perhaps the window, where Kathleen had appeared before, transparent enough for Meredith to see the floral curtains through her floating image.

But no matter how hard she strained to see something, Kathleen's apparition failed to appear.

She got up and wandered over to the painting on the

wall. Kathleen had pointed directly at it. But there were no weeds in the painting. Only flowers. Great, huge clusters of them, dotted with butterflies.

Meredith turned away. In the next instant she caught her breath. Once more she studied the painting. Among the brilliant hues the colorful butterflies hovered and perched on the petals of white daisies.

Meredith closed her eyes. She saw again Amelia's hat sitting on the dresser. White lace daisies. *Tiny, colorful butterflies*.

With a heavy sigh Meredith sat back down on her bed. Maybe that's what Kathleen was trying to tell her after all.

Seething with anger over the humiliation she'd suffered in front of the class, Amelia might well have followed Kathleen outside, bent on revenge.

It was difficult to imagine the young woman striking the teacher with that heavy branch. Then again, when driven by such powerful emotions, anything was possible.

Again Meredith closed her eyes. If she had done so, no wonder Kathleen had been so agitated. It would have devastated her to know she had died at the hands of a beloved student.

Somehow, Meredith promised herself, she'd have to find out for sure if Amelia was responsible, and if so, to make that young woman pay for the crime. Though how she was going to do that was a mystery. Amelia Webster was an accomplished liar, and all Meredith had for evidence was the word of a ghost. Not exactly something she could take to the police.

Especially since P.C. Shipham was so reluctant to take anything she said seriously. He'd really have a belly laugh or two when she tried to explain how she came to suspect Amelia of the crime.

There was only one way she could know for sure if Amelia was guilty and bring her to justice. She would have to make the girl confess.

It seemed an impossible task, but Meredith had faced impossible odds before and managed to overcome them. Somehow she would find a way.

"I promise you, Kathleen," she whispered. "If Amelia did this to you, I'll see she pays."

She slept fitfully that night and awoke to discover she had overslept. When she arrived at the assembly hall, breathless and feeling out of sorts, Felicity was delivering the morning address.

Sylvia looked down her nose at her as she slipped onto her chair on the stage, and Meredith responded with a bright smile. The new teacher looked away, her lips pursed in disapproval.

That would be another black mark in her book, Meredith thought, with a flare of resentment. No doubt to be duly reported to Stuart Hamilton. It was really tiresome to have an informant in their midst.

She wouldn't put it past the man to have deliberately placed Sylvia at Bellehaven for the express purpose of spying on her performance as headmistress.

In the next moment she was ashamed of her unwarranted suspicions. Sylvia was simply one of those women who took it upon herself to observe and expose any sign of incompetence or failure. While, no doubt, considering herself above reproach.

It was hard to befriend a woman like that, but if there was to be any harmony between the instructresses, as there must be for a school to be managed effectively, then she would have to find some way to bring Sylvia into the fold, so to speak, and make her feel a member of the team instead of an outsider. No mean task.

So absorbed was she in the dilemma, she failed to realize Felicity had finished the morning address. Taken by surprise, she was left seated on her chair while everyone else rose to their feet for the prayer.

She jumped up so suddenly she caught the edge of the seat with the back of her knees. It toppled backward with an almighty crash.

Giggles rippled across the hall as she bent over to retrieve the pesky thing and set it upright. She straightened, and met Sylvia's condemning gaze full on.

Drat the woman. Hamilton was going to have an entire list of her faults to gloat over by the end of the day.

Annoyed to find the vexing man in her thoughts once more, she looked at Felicity, who also stared at her as if she'd lost her mind. "Please proceed," Meredith said, with as much dignity as she could muster.

Felicity gave a slight shake of her head, then began reading the prayer.

Meredith drew a long sigh of relief when she was free at last to leave the stage and retire to her classroom.

Chapter 17

The morning dragged for Meredith. The students were restless and less attentive than normal, and she had trouble concentrating on the life and times of John Constable . . . one of her favorite landscape painters.

By the time the bell sounded she was only too happy to leave the class and go back to her office, where the accounts waited. Even then she found it hard to focus on the neatly written figures. The memory of Kathleen's despairing face kept floating into her mind, blotting out everything else.

When the bell rang for the midday meal, she was startled out of yet another reverie, with less than half of her work completed. Worse, she was no closer to solving the problem of how to force a possible confession out of Amelia Webster.

It seemed as if Kathleen might be doomed to wander around the grounds of Bellehaven, seeking a justice that would forever be denied her.

Heavy of heart, Meredith made her way to the dining

hall. The plate of lamb stew Olivia put in front of her failed to excite her appetite, and she had barely touched it when she dismissed the students at her table.

Leaving the dining hall, she made her way to the teacher's lounge, uncharitably hoping that Sylvia would not be there. At least that wish was granted, since Felicity and Essie sat alone by the window, discussing the afternoon's curriculum.

They both looked up as Meredith entered, concern visible on both their faces.

"You look dreadful," Felicity observed with her usual candor. "Are you ill?"

"Just a little tired." Meredith sank onto a chair next to them. "I didn't sleep well last night."

Felicity's gaze sharpened. "Kathleen been visiting you again?"

"No," Meredith looked down at her hands lying restlessly in her lap. "I rather wish she had."

"Is something worrying you, Meredith?" Essie leaned forward, her soft blue eyes anxiously scouring Meredith's face. "You don't seem yourself at all."

"That's an understatement." Felicity frowned at her. "You're letting this business with Kathleen destroy your own health. Let it go, Meredith. Kathleen is dead. You have a life to live, and people who rely on you. You can't allow a dead woman to interfere with that, no matter how close you were to her. Keep this up and you're liable to lose your position, your home here, everything."

"I can't let it rest." Meredith lifted her hands and let them drop again. "Kathleen won't let me. She'll follow me around and haunt me until I bring her killer to justice. I'm quite sure of it."

Felicity growled in disgust. "Really Meredith, you must

be strong. You've done your best to find out who killed her. The task is just too difficult. Kathleen must understand that." She shook her head, mumbling, "I still can't believe we are sitting here talking about Kathleen as if she were still alive."

Essie reached out and laid her cool hand over Meredith's fingers. "Felicity's right," she murmured. "This whole business is making you ill. We don't like to see you like this. You are usually so strong and unperturbed."

"I don't feel in the least bit strong and unperturbed." Wearily, Meredith stroked her forehead with her fingers. "I should tell you, however, that I believe I might have found out who killed Kathleen. I just don't know how to prove it."

Both women stared at her openmouthed. Felicity was the first to speak. "Who is it? How did you . . ."

"Oh, my goodness." Essie's eyes were wide above her trembling hand. "Is it someone we know?"

With a calmness she didn't feel inside, Meredith related her thought process of the night before. "I felt from the first that Amelia was unusually upset over Kathleen's death," she finished. "Especially in light of the fact she'd been so humiliated in front of the class. I just didn't put everything together until last night."

"But you still don't know for a fact it was Amelia," Felicity said, sounding doubtful.

"No, I don't." Meredith sighed. "And I have no way of proving it one way or another, save getting her to confess, and I really don't see how I can do that."

"It's a pity that you seem to be the only one who can see Kathleen's ghost," Essie said. "Perhaps if Kathleen could appear in front of Amelia, it would frighten her enough to admit what she's done."

"If she did it," Felicity reminded her.

"I'm as sure as I can be that she did." Meredith got up from the chair. "All of Kathleen's clues point to it. The flowers, the weeds, the butterflies . . . all of it."

"Well, I can just imagine Constable Shipham's response to that."

Meredith shook her head. "I just don't know what to do next. I'm going to take a walk around the grounds. Maybe it will clear my head."

Essie jumped to her feet. "I'll go with you."

"No, thank you." Meredith smiled to soften her words. "I really want to be alone for a while."

Though she seemed disappointed, Essie merely nodded and sat back down.

As Meredith reached the door she heard Felicity murmur, "Give our regards to Kathleen."

Essie uttered a sound of protest, but ignoring them both, Meredith opened the door and walked out of the room.

Once outside, Meredith walked briskly across the courtyard and followed the long curving path down to the gates. The breeze cooled her face, though the sunlight filtering through the trees failed to lift her spirits.

In another month the leaves would be turning, and the woods would be bathed in gold, yellow, and crimson hues. There was something more than a little sad about autumn. She hated saying farewell to the long, warm summer days, and dreaded the cruel winds of winter ahead.

Bellehaven was so cold and drafty in the winter, the only way to keep warm was to huddle over the fires that burned in every fireplace. She dreaded the extra layer of clothes needed to be comfortable.

She loathed the icy sheets on the bed at night, the frost inside the windows, the snow piling up in drifts so high it was impossible to walk to the village.

How wonderful it must be to live in a warm climate, to anticipate the sun every day, enjoy tropical nights and warm sea breezes. In the heart of the dark, dreary English winters she'd read about such places and felt a longing deep in her soul.

A longing unlikely to be satisfied, she thought wistfully, as she retraced her steps back to the school. Then again, how ungrateful was she to resent her situation. At least she was alive—unlike Kathleen, who'd had her life snatched from her in such a brutal manner.

No matter how harsh the winters were, she could still enjoy roasted chestnuts, ice skating on the pond, and the Christmas season, with its special kind of magic all around.

While poor Kathleen floated around on the outside, belonging to neither this world nor the next. Waiting for her best friend to set her free.

"I tried, Kathleen." Meredith lifted her chin to the sky. "I really tried. I'm so sorry I let you down." When she lowered her face again it was wet with tears.

It was much later in the day when the idea came to her. After supper she had gone back to her office to finish the bookkeeping she had neglected earlier.

Her eyelids were heavy and drooping by the time she finally closed the last ledger. She sat at her desk for several minutes, letting the weariness take over her. All being well, she told herself, she would sleep better tonight.

The seconds ticked by on the clock, until at last she stirred, stretched, and rose to her feet. If Kathleen should pay her a visit this night, she would be too deep in sleep to see her.

She smiled, remembering Essie's words from that afternoon. *Perhaps if Kathleen could appear in front of Amelia, it would frighten her enough to admit what she's done.*

After gently closing the door of her office, she headed for the stairs. Halfway up them she paused. Of course. She should have thought of it before. With renewed hope, she continued on her way.

Amelia Webster had not slept well for the past week or so. Although she fell sleep within minutes, it was to endure disturbing nightmares such as monsters chasing her, flames leaping from their deadly claws. After which she would awaken, drenched in sweat yet chilled to the bone.

This night was no exception. The monsters in her dream had come so close she could feel the heat from their breath, yet when she awoke, her entire body shook with cold.

Reaching out, she took hold of the eiderdown and dragged it up under her chin. The chill seemed to penetrate the mound of soft feathers.

Turning on her side, she peered at the bed next to hers. In the shadows cast by the moonlight she could see the flattened covers quite clearly. Frowning, she stared harder. Loretta was not in her bed.

Amelia sat up, hauling the eiderdown up over her shoulders. Loretta had been in her bed earlier. They had talked for a while before falling asleep. Where could she be?

Sighing, Amelia slid down onto her pillow again. She must have slipped out again to meet her boyfriend. After Mrs. Llewellyn had expressly forbidden her. She'd be sent home in disgrace, if she didn't take care. Loretta had whined about Mrs. Llewellyn's warning all through supper.

Well, if she wanted to risk being expelled, that was her

business. Amelia turned on her side and closed her eyes. She had enough to worry about without concerning herself about Loretta's problems.

Doing her best to shut out the thoughts crowding her mind, she concentrated on getting back to sleep.

A slight sound barely penetrated her conscience. It was only the wind blowing branches against the window, she told herself. But, a moment or two later she heard it again—a scraping noise. No, a rustling. Like skirts brushing against the dresser.

It had to be Loretta, come back and creeping into bed. She no doubt hoped her friend was asleep and hadn't noticed her absence.

Quietly Amelia turned over, intent on scaring the daylights out of her. "What do you think you are doing?" she demanded, in her best imitation of Mrs. Llewellyn's sharp tones.

But Loretta was not standing by the bed. She was over by the dresser, and she looked quite different. Much taller, and . . . Amelia swallowed. She looked as if she had no head. Only a white, swaying body with waving arms.

Convinced she was having another nightmare, Amelia pinched herself. It hurt. She stared at the figure, her mouth dry. It was hard to see in the faint glow of moonlight, but she could swear there was no head.

She shut her eyes tight, then carefully opened them, praying the strange figure would be gone. Not only was it still there, it moved toward her.

Shrinking back, Amelia cried out in a voice that sounded nothing like her own. "Who are you? What do you want?"

The creature halted, but it swayed from side to side, uttering a dreadful moan that filled Amelia with cold, chilling dread.

"Go away!" she shouted, clutching the eiderdown for protection. "Go away or I'll scream for the teachers."

The figure lifted its arms and moaned again. Then, in a weird, quavering voice, it spoke. "Vengeance. I want vengeance."

Amelia drew her knees up under her chin. Her teeth chattered so badly she could hardly speak. "Go away! I don't know who you are. I don't know what you want with me."

"You do know who I am. I'm Miss Duncan." The figure moaned again. "I'm here to punish the one who killed me."

Tears spurted from Amelia's eyes and rolled down her chin. "Oh, no! I didn't mean to kill you. I was angry with you. You made me look like a fool in front of the class and I followed you that night to tell you how angry that made me. But when I called out your name you just kept walking away. That made me even more angry that you wouldn't listen to me." Giving in to the sobs that shook her body, she buried her face in her arms.

"You killed me," the figure moaned. "You must face your punishment."

"I d-d-didn't mean t-to!" Amelia fought hard to get out the words. "I know I lost my temper and picked up the branch. I didn't mean to hit you with it. I wanted to throw it in front of you to make you stop and listen. B-b-ut it was heavy. It hit you instead. I tried to wake you up. I really d-did. But then I got scared and ran back to school. I'm s-s-sorry." Once more she let the sobs take over.

Dimly she heard the scrape of a match, then light glowed all around her. Cautiously she opened her eyes. Standing in front of her, a glimmering oil lamp in one hand and a white sheet in the other, was Mrs. Llewellyn.

"So," Felicity said, "you pretended to be Kathleen's ghost. How creative."

"It really was clever of you, Meredith." Essie reached out to the vase of chrysanthemums on the table, and re-arranged some of the flowers. "I'm sure I wouldn't have thought of it."

"Actually, it was you who gave me the idea." Meredith leaned back with a sigh. She had asked Felicity and Essie to meet her in the library before breakfast so they could discuss what to do about Amelia.

Last night she had been angry enough with the girl to want her taken away in handcuffs, but now that she'd had time to sleep on it she had to acknowledge that the tragedy was more of a dreadful accident than murder.

Yet Amelia was at fault, even if her intention wasn't to harm Kathleen, and some sort of punishment was merited.

"Me?" Essie's surprised exclamation broke into Mere-dith's thoughts. "How did I give you the idea?"

"When you said it was a pity Amelia couldn't see Kath-leen's ghost. That's when I decided to let her think she was indeed seeing the ghost."

"But a sheet," Felicity said, shaking her head. "How on earth did you get away with that?"

"Moonlight." Meredith smiled. "It plays tricks with your eyes. Also, Amelia's guilt made it easier for her to be-lieve she really was seeing Kathleen."

"I suppose." Felicity yawned. "What are you going to do now?"

"That's what I want to discuss with you." Meredith looked at each of her friends. "What do you suggest I do?"

"Well, expel her from school of course. We can't have a pupil with that vicious a temper running around threatening everyone who gets in her way."

"I agree." Essie shuddered. "I should be too nervous to ever chastise her again, in case she comes after me with a tree branch."

"I'd already decided to do that. We shall have to tell her parents why she is being sent home, of course. But what concerns me is the fact that P.C. Shipham should be informed."

"Oh, dear." Essie's face creased in concern. "Do we have to? I mean, she didn't mean to kill Kathleen by all accounts. I hate the thought of such a young woman being dragged into court and perhaps put in prison."

"Nevertheless, she was responsible for the death of her tutor." Meredith hesitated, reluctant to pursue the matter yet knowing she must. "Whether it was carelessness, bad judgment, or uncontrollable temper, she has to answer to that."

"Absolutely." Felicity lifted her hand in a fist. "Justice must prevail. After all, isn't that why Kathleen tried so hard to tell us who killed her? She needed justice to go . . . wherever we go when we die."

"Essie?" Meredith held out a hand in appeal. "Surely you agree?"

Essie looked most unhappy, but reluctantly inclined her head. "I suppose so. Such an awful pity, though. She's a bright girl and I really hate to see such great promise go to waste."

"Well, maybe it won't be a waste. Perhaps the courts

will go lightly on her and she will have learned her lesson and will control her temper from now on."

"That's my Meredith," Felicity said cheerfully. "Always looking on the positive side of things."

"Do you think Kathleen is satisfied now?" Essie looked wistfully out of the window. "Do you think she's crossed over to the other world?"

"I hope so." Meredith followed her gaze. "But I'll miss her. Although I couldn't communicate directly with her, it was comforting in a way to know she was still with us."

"Well, I certainly hope she has gone." Felicity surged to her feet. "Perhaps now you can stop looking like a ghost yourself and find some peace. Get some color back in your cheeks. Really, Meredith, you've looked positively haggard these past few days."

Meredith winced. Trust Felicity to put some reality into the conversation. "I think we should all go to breakfast," she said, rising to her feet. "I'm absolutely ravenous."

"That's the most invigorating thing you've said all morning." Felicity strode to the door. "Last one in the dining hall is a sissy."

Amelia's parents arrived that afternoon and were astounded to hear that their daughter had been responsible for the death of a teacher. P.C. Shipham arrived an hour later, and seemed not at all grateful that Meredith had solved the mystery of Kathleen's demise.

After explaining to the Websters the necessity of a court case, he took a tearful Amelia into custody. As they were leaving, he couldn't resist a parting shot.

"I do hope, Mrs. Llewellyn," he said, as Meredith accompanied them to the main doors, "that you will not make a habit of sticking your nose in business that doesn't concern you. You were lucky this time. Next time it could be a dangerous murderer."

"I sincerely hope that it won't be necessary for me to track down another killer," Meredith assured him. "I would hate to see anyone else struck down like that."

Shipham looked down his nose at her. "They won't be, as long as they don't go walking about after dark by theirselves."

"However," Meredith continued, "should something that unfortunate occur, I can assure you, Constable, I shall pursue the matter with as much fervor and determination as I have done for Miss Duncan."

The constable's face darkened. "One of these days, mark my word, you'll be sorry you said that."

She watched him lead Amelia down the steps, followed by her anxious parents. She felt sorry for the young woman. Life would be difficult for her for a while.

She was preparing to retire that evening when to her utter dismay, she felt the room grow icy cold. Standing by her bed, she froze. Surely Kathleen could not still be here. For a moment she panicked. Had she made a mistake? But no, Amelia had confessed. It had all been explained.

Hoping it was merely her imagination, she turned toward the window. No, she hadn't imagined it. For there was the cloud, with Kathleen's figure slowly materializing in the middle of it.

"It was Amelia," Meredith said sharply. "It's all been taken care of, Kathleen. You can go in peace now. Justice will be served."

The apparition grew stronger, and now she could see Kathleen's face. There was something else, though. Something different about the shape of Kathleen's body.

Staring at the odd vision forming at her late friend's side, Meredith blinked, and blinked again. She was not mistaken. Standing at Kathleen's side, just as transparent and elusive, was the figure of a child.

Meredith looked up at Kathleen's face, but already she was fading. Ghostly hands pushed the child's figure toward her, then Kathleen was gone.

Meredith knew in that instant that she would see her friend no more. Kathleen, however, had left a parting gift. For the gossamer figure of the child remained, looking up at her, hands stretched out in appeal.

Meredith sank onto her bed. It would seem she was not done with ghosts after all. She looked at the child, cringing at the thought of what lie ahead. "All right, my precious," she said softly. "Now what's your story?"